WE WERE LUCKY
WITH THE RAIN

WE WERE LUCKY WITH THE RAIN

stories

Susan Buttenwieser

Four Way Books
Tribeca

For Andy and my daughters

Library of Congress Cataloging-in-Publication Data

Names: Buttenwieser, Susan, author.
Title: We were lucky with the rain : stories / Susan Buttenwieser.
Description: Tribeca : Four Way Books, [2020] | Identifiers: LCCN 2019054709 |
ISBN 9781945588556 (trade paperback ; acid-free paper)
Classification: LCC PS3602.U8924 A6 2020 | DDC 813/.6--dc23
LC record available at https://lccn.loc.gov/2019054709

This book is manufactured in the United States of America and printed on
acid-free paper.

Four Way Books is a not-for-profit literary press. We are grateful for the assistance
we receive from individual donors, public arts agencies, and private foundations.

This publication is made possible with public funds from the
New York State Council on the Arts, a state agency.

We are a proud member of the Community of Literary Magazines and Presses.

Contents

Translucent Ghosts

STANLEY SITS ON A BENCH just outside the Lionel Street playground watching Leslie and her daughters. By now, he has memorized their entire after-school routine, which has remained virtually unchanged since he started following them several months ago.

Mondays they go to Mrs. Wiggan's Ballet Studio. Tuesdays are the Newman Square Library Story Hour and then a grocery run at Price Chopper. Unless it's raining, Wednesdays and Thursdays are always spent here at this playground. And Fridays they go to the Eastside Y for Polliwog and Guppy swim classes and then on to dinner at Luigi's Pizzeria with Leslie's husband and another family.

Even though the morning was fairly mild, it has degenerated into a brisk, fall afternoon, the kind that comes on by surprise. Strong blasts of wind send brown maple leaves torpedoing through the park. Leslie has taken up her usual spot, perched on a worn-out picnic table surrounded by six other moms pulling their too-thin jackets tightly around themselves. She seems to know everyone at the playground, greeting children and their caregivers by name in her invariably exuberant manner. Her younger daughter is in the sandbox making castles with the same sullen-faced boy that she's always with. The older girl is up on the jungle gym, then on the monkey bars, a constant swirl of kids trying to keep up with her.

One of the mothers comes back from a coffee run, and the women clutch the paper cups and talk furiously, their hands gesticulating. Occasionally someone says something funny and they all laugh.

Stanley met Leslie at her Labor Day family barbecue. A woman he dated briefly had brought him along. It was a hot day, and Stanley spent his time in the air-conditioned basement watching a baseball game with a group of men who were avoiding the heat and their families. At one point during the long afternoon, he had helped Leslie open a large bottle of chardonnay and it turned out they both shared an affinity for guacamole.

He spotted her coming out of Price Chopper a few weeks later, wheeling a large cart through the parking lot with her two daughters hanging off it. He called out to her, but she didn't respond, so he got closer and tried again. Still nothing. Realizing that she hadn't even seen him, he crouched behind a car and watched her unload bags of groceries into the back of a blue station wagon, hand each girl a colored plastic snack container, talking to them in that singsong, pretend-happy parent voice. As she reversed out of the parking space, she rolled down her window and he could hear children's music wafting out. There was something fascinating and also, he had to admit to himself, slightly comforting about this, and Stanley felt an overwhelming urge to find out where they were going next. He hurried towards his own car, which had belonged to his mother, and drove after them.

Stanley pulls out his Thought Journal and scans the playground. Human resources has assigned a social worker to the content monitoring department in the wake of Ted Farley's recent suicide. Now, every Wednesday morning, Stanley and his co-workers have to extract themselves from their cubicles and the endless stream of videos that they watch to ensure that snuff films, child pornography, and anything else illegal doesn't make it onto the file-sharing website. After helping themselves to coffee and mini muffins, they sit around the large white conference table while the social worker writes things down on a flip chart. Sometimes, she circles a word in the middle of the paper and they are supposed to come up with one that relates to it. One session involved learning improvisation. Another was spent on deep breathing techniques and visualizing waterfalls. And yesterday, they worked on a collaborative art project.

The social worker distributed composition notebooks on her first day. "These are Thought Journals and you should use them to keep track of any increases in anxiety, sleep problems, or depression," she'd instructed. "You should also record emotional responses to disturbing images. And I find writing down dreams helpful. Just FYI."

Their jobs are now classified as high-risk, Keith Orlanski reported later on in the break room, as if he had inside information. His theory is that if they can demonstrate workplace-related trauma or permanent psychological damage, they might be eligible for disability. This caused quite a commotion. "Kind of a gamble, don't you think? Hard to get a contract renewed if they think you're looney tunes," Mona Tucker said firmly. "Just FYI." Most people seemed to agree and went back to quietly eating from the free snacks tray.

HR also pushed the company's onsite gym and flex-time policy. Stanley used the opportunity to change his work schedule so that he could be there right when Leslie picked up her daughters from school. "It's wonderful to see fathers who are so involved with their kids," his supervisor said when Stanley asked about working the 6:30 a.m. to 2:30 p.m. shift. Like most of his co-workers, he was on a short-term contract and kept his personal life to himself. There seemed no good reason to tell her that in fact he didn't have children.

Stanley starts to work on this week's assignment: write down five vivid childhood memories. But he can think of only one. Instead of going with his son to Little League or ice hockey games like the other fathers in the neighborhood, Stanley's took him birding on Saturday mornings. They were up before sunrise, and the kitchen was always cold at that hour, even in summer. Stanley would sit at their green Formica table eating Froot Loops, watching his father fill up a thermos with fresh-brewed coffee before they set off. They'd listen to sports radio while they drove through dark, empty streets and out to the lake.

If he closes his eyes, Stanley can still recall the way the lake looked when the early morning began to explode with light. The best place to see birds was from a partially rotted dock overlooking a marsh. They'd sit there quietly together, binoculars affixed to their faces, watching ducks, Canada geese, cardinals, and robins, his father pointing excitedly if they saw the blue heron gliding just above the water. The fishing boats slept in the deeper part of the lake where the trout and bass were, so the only human sound was his father sipping coffee from the thermos and clearing his throat. If they managed to get to the lake extra early, they'd catch the barn owls still out and flying around, their underbellies lit up like translucent ghosts.

Stanley looks up from his journal just as two boys run at top speed right through the elaborate sand city that Leslie's younger daughter has been working on the whole time they have been at the playground. The sullen-faced boy screams, grabs a fistful of sand and chases after them. Several nearby adults swoop into action, rousing themselves off their cell phones to intervene. Somehow during the commotion, Leslie's daughter gets stepped on and begins to wail.

At first Leslie doesn't realize what's going on and Stanley has to stifle the urge to call out to her. Finally, one of the mothers alerts her and Leslie rushes to her daughter, picks her up and holds her. The girl's small shoulders rack with sobs. Leslie settles her on her lap and pats her back, gives her something to drink from a sippy cup. She checks her watch and seems to decide that it's time to go home, which makes the girl cry even harder. Leslie continues to soothe her, whispering something reassuring, and eventually she calms down and goes to find her shoes. It takes a bit more persuading to pry the older one away from her friends. They gather up their backpacks and coats, wave goodbye to most of the playground before piling into their station wagon.

Stanley trails behind Leslie, changing into the left-hand lane on Walnut Drive. When they reach her neighborhood, which is quiet and residential, Stanley lets a few cars get between his and the station wagon, just to be safe. Only another mile and a half and they'll be on Sylvian Road. Home.

The Check Engine light has been on ever since he inherited the car from his mother. She had Alzheimer's for years but ended up dying of lung cancer exactly one year ago. Her obituary in the Allendale Nursing Home newsletter reported that she'd died after a courageous battle with cancer and Stanley imagined his mother as a ten-foot tall gladiator with a sword instead of the stooped woman who barely got out of bed, talked only to herself, and hadn't recognized her own son in years. Stanley was the only immediate family at her small memorial service; he had no siblings and his father died when Stanley was in high school. There were no other close relatives. A few women who used to play bridge with Stanley's mother before she lost her memory helped put together a reception in the function room at First Presbyterian. Some former neighbors brought ham salad sandwiches, a cheese platter, and fruit trays. The minister sat with Stanley after bringing him a cup of coffee and a napkin filled with store bought cookies, and women that Stanley mostly didn't recognize took turns coming over to give him their condolences.

Up ahead he can see the station wagon turning onto her road, a cul-de-sac that dead-ends at the woods. He idles at the corner while she pulls into the second driveway on the right.

Even this far away he can hear their dog barking and jumping against the kitchen door. The girls bolt out of the back seat and rush inside their two-story Craftsman. He waits until Leslie has followed them into the house before parking directly across the street, like he does most afternoons.

Lights come on in the kitchen but only the outlines of their bodies are visible through the large window overlooking the front lawn. But it's hard to tell from his car exactly what they are doing.

Leslie's husband won't be back for at least another hour, and Stanley just likes to sit in his car awhile, right outside the house. He thinks of the social worker's instructions for what she calls "sense-memory" writing. "Close your eyes and think of your five senses," she said during this week's session. "Take them in before you do your writing. Then pick a room from your childhood. Your bedroom, the kitchen, wherever you watched TV. The room you spent the most time in. What did this room smell like? What sounds could you hear? What do you remember eating when you were in this room? What did it look like? How did you feel in this room?"

Stanley leans back against the headrest in his mother's pale blue Oldsmobile and closes his eyes. The car seat is cotton and stained with years of spilled Tab. Crumbs fill the crevices and it still smells of his mother's cigarettes even though it has been years since she was behind the wheel. His mother sold his childhood home right after his father died, moved them to a condo in the center of town, and bought this car. As hard as he tries, he can't recall much about the home where he grew up, a modest, two-bedroom ranch house.

Stanley doesn't have a real kitchen where he lives now, an apartment complex that used to be a motel until it was converted into rental units. The developers didn't bother to put in large appliances, instead supplementing the spare rooms with hot plates and mini-fridges. The only evidence of its holiday-destination past is an empty, leaf-strewn pool in the courtyard. On warm evenings, Stanley sits out on the small balcony overlooking it. He hasn't actually cooked anything since he moved in, sticking with cold cereal for breakfast and take-out from the fast-food places across the street.

A few weeks ago, the social worker assigned describing a favorite childhood meal, and Stanley had followed Leslie into Price Chopper, hoping to discover what her family ate. He worried she would notice him and didn't get close enough to see what was in her cart. But he could tell that Leslie was the type who makes a couple of dishes on Sunday afternoons that she freezes for later on in the week, lasagna, maybe, or chili, the kitchen permanently filled with the scent of baking chocolate chip cookies, slowly simmering stew, breakfast sausages on Sundays.

Stanley longs to be closer to Leslie and her daughters, to stand in their flowerbeds where she has already planted bulbs for the spring and press his face against the window and watch them in this before-dinner time. Or to be right there inside with the three of them, hear the jazz playing from the public radio station, the dog going at its bone, the girls arguing playfully while they do their homework, Leslie saying occasionally, "Settle down," while she chops vegetables on a wooden cutting board. See the kitchen walls overcrowded with children's artwork, the refrigerator smothered with family photographs and school memos in a cluttered yet generally organized way, and by the stove, those labeled ceramic containers of flour, sugar, coffee, and one for brown sugar with a folded-up paper towel on top to keep the moisture in. Like his mother used to have.

Slowly, he opens the car door and steps into the quiet hush of late afternoon. Light spills out from the houses onto front lawns all up and down the street in the post-daylight savings darkness. No one else is outside.

He crosses the street and stands in their driveway breathing in the crisp fresh air that smells of bagged-up leaves and smoke from a nearby fireplace. A sliver of the new moon is visible behind the trees.

Looking around one last time just to make sure no one can see him, he crouches and quietly shuffles toward the moving shapes in Leslie's kitchen. A jack-o-lantern is on the stoop of their front door. The jagged smile twists downward, sagging with decay, beckoning Stanley forward.

Someone's Drunk Wife

SOMEONE'S DRUNK WIFE is in an upstairs bedroom. She has been flirting with you for hours and now the party is over. Her husband is not here. You sit in a chair while your friend gets you pillows and sheets, spreads them out on the floor. Someone else has already passed out on the couch.

"Are you sure you'll be okay here?" your friend asks. You are not so sure, but you are better off here in the living room than upstairs with her.

You are at that in-between stage, too drunk to drive home, but not drunk enough to sleep with someone's drunk wife. Even though there is a thick carpet on the floor, it's hard to find a comfortable position. First you lie on your back but feel stiff after only a few minutes. Then you try your left side, but that's much worse. You get up and go to the bathroom in the hallway, right by the staircase. Light is visible from under the door in the guest room where she's staying.

You go outside to have a cigarette on the patio. It is just starting to get light, the sky a washed-out brown. Maybe you aren't too drunk, maybe you could drive home.

Your friend who had the party has a large house, professionally decorated, with a pool in the backyard. You met him years ago, back when you were both struggling comedy writers in New York. Now he's the showrunner for an Emmy-winning comedy and you write spec scripts, take meetings, and do short-term writing jobs. The party was a surprise to celebrate his fortieth birthday that his wife threw for him. Their new baby is in the room next to where the drunken wife is. More rooms are filled with other party guests, also too drunk to drive home. If you'd just gone to sleep a little earlier, maybe you would be in an actual bed right now, instead of having to choose between the floor and adultery.

Everywhere in the house are framed photographs of your friend with his wife. Since the baby was born, tasteful black and whites of the three of them have been added to the collection. Pictures of your friend with various celebrities cover the walls in his study. The only photos you have are on your refrigerator, your older sister's Christmas card from last year with your twin nieces sitting underneath a wreath and one from the year before of them sitting on a pony. If you open the door too quickly, they come flying off, and you have to search around on your hands and knees to find the magnets that hold them up.

Maybe you are drunk enough to sleep with someone's drunk wife.

You have another cigarette and decide to try to drive home. It's not that far after all, you reason as you pass through the hallway. The light in the guest room is off now anyway. You walk down the driveway to your car parked out on the street and sit in it, but you're having trouble getting the key in the ignition. "This is stupid," you say out loud. You crawl into the back and shove all the crap from the seat onto the floor. Then you lie down and curl into the fetal position.

The night had started hopefully enough. First you talked to a woman that you'd met about a month before at another party. You were having a good time together when her boyfriend showed up. She didn't seem that happy to see him either, but still, there he was. So, you hung out with your friend for a while, long enough to be introduced to a producer who was trying to find a bathroom. He's hiring writers for a new show and your friend managed to get you a meeting with him. Then a woman you'd seen around started talking with you and your friend. You were feeling optimistic when you went to have a cigarette with her alone on the glider swing. But she started getting weird about an ex-boyfriend. Finally, her friend came and got her.

When you were ordering another drink from the bartender, you met someone's drunk wife. From then on, she was all over you, asking questions about your career, where you grew up, school, your family, everything, as if you were the most interesting guy she'd ever met. She went to college with your friend and his wife, and through jokes and things, you found out that she was from out of town, staying here for the whole weekend. No one said why her husband wasn't with her.

After a while, everyone else either went home or to bed and it was just you, your friend, a couple, and someone's drunk wife. When you all moved inside and sat around the kitchen island and had that one last drink, she took your hand and held onto it. The couple started bickering about going home. The husband was pulling out a baggie of cocaine when his wife made him leave before it turned into that kind of an evening. The drunk wife was stroking your fingers, so you asked your friend if maybe you could stay over. Maybe you shouldn't drive home, you'd said. You waited for the drunk wife to do something.

But she started drinking glasses of water in an attempt to get rid of her hiccups and talking with your friend about their summer vacation. Then she was saying goodnight and heading up to bed, your friend was getting sheets out of a linen closet and you were sleeping on the floor, alone.

You are starting to doze off in your car. It is daylight now and the next-door neighbors come out to retrieve the Sunday paper, walk their dog. You wake up several hours later baking in the backseat and walk up the steep driveway. Everyone is sprawled out in the lush backyard, eating breakfast. "Hey." Your friend winks at you. "We were wondering what happened to you."

The drunk wife is sober now, swimming in the pool with your friend's wife and the baby, talking to her husband on her phone, and you are relieved. It would have been that too-drunk-to-have-sex sex, the kind where you can barely feel it when you come. And then what would you have done? Woken up wrapped around each other?

You slept with someone's wife before. Actually, it was kind of an affair, with her calling you hurriedly whenever her husband wasn't around, having sex wherever you could. The best sex you ever had in your whole life, but it was crazy. She was always crying afterwards, and you could never do anything normal, like see a movie or meet for a drink. Just have amazing sex in weird places. Her husband found out and you ended up crying too when she told you she couldn't see you anymore. You think about her from time to time, wondering what would have happened if only you had admitted you were in love with her.

The two women wave at you from the swimming pool as they pass the baby back and forth. Last night, you didn't sleep with someone's drunk wife. It had been a close call, but everything is okay now.

If You Lived Here, You'd Be Home Now

KATIE'S MOTHER FELL FOR DENNIS in the aftermath of Tropical Storm Bonnie. They were both Red Cross volunteers, and they kept seeing each other as more natural disasters followed. Most of the hurricane season was spent together, coordinating meals and emergency shelters. After Hurricane Matthew struck five months later, Rose decided to leave Boston where she had lived her entire life, move to Florida, and marry Dennis.

Now Katie waits in Terminal A at Logan International as the rising sun glints off the airplanes scattered around the tarmac. It is a crisp spring morning and a never-used suit carrier, which she bought in anticipation of job interviews in distant locations that never happened, rests against her legs. Inside, all folded up, is her only wedding-appropriate dress, which she will wear later today. The man next to her is on his cell phone, closing his mother's bank account and claiming her life insurance policy because she just died. Katie tries to stay focused on her newspaper, but finds herself listening in on his conversations, glancing over at the notebook spread out on his lap with intricate lists and phone numbers. Methodically, without emotion, he checks things off after each call. Then there's an announcement that it's time to board the plane.

Her mother started volunteering with the Red Cross almost fifteen years ago, right after Katie's father died from a heart attack. Katie was a senior in high school, her older brother and sister had already moved away, and her mother wanted something to get her out of the house in the evening. Obstructed breathing and CPR training became Rose's specialty. She even had her own Resusci Annie and baby dolls, which lay side by side in the back of the station wagon. Then she switched to Disaster Services, getting on the hurricane circuit, following storms around the country.

When Katie lands in Fort Myers, her older brother is idling outside the terminal in a white rental car that smells of stale chewing gum and a hint of vomit.

"I hate Florida," Vincent says, as they sit in midday traffic.

"But you've lived here twice."

"That's different."

If you throw a dart on a map of the United States, Vincent has probably lived in a nearby city where he knows at least eight good bars. He works as a session musician and moves suddenly and often, prompted by his horoscope, an email from a long-lost friend, sidewalk graffiti. In the past two years alone, Vincent has lived in Nashville, Seattle, Austin, and now L.A., where he's been for a whole six months. It's his fifth move to the city, motivated this time by passing a homeless man crossing the street muttering, "Sometimes you have to ad lib." Vincent went home, packed his bags and was gone within hours.

Katie has never lived outside the greater Boston area where she grew up and has spent the past decade in and out of the Mass College of Art. Finally, she got her graduate degree last year but could only find a job at Fun Town, a children's play space, in Medford. Instead of teaching, Katie spends her days dressed like a clown and overseeing preschool craft projects: popsicle stick sculpture, gluing Cheerios and dry pasta onto paper plates, making pipe cleaner dolls.

She just moved to a new sublet in Brighton with three other women that she doesn't know very well. They communicate with each other mostly through angry Post-It notes about the bills and masking tape labels on their individual Tupperware containers of food in the refrigerator.

The traffic eases up when Vincent and Katie reach a narrow beach access road crowded with bait shops, motels, and seafood restaurants on either side. They decide to stop at a seafood shack called Barnacle Bill's, which has real money covering the walls. Customers help themselves to the stapler inside the kitchen, adding a dollar to the collage once they've finished their meal.

A girl with braces hands them their order number and they sit at a picnic table overlooking a canal while they wait for their fried fish sandwiches. Sea grass shoots up through the wooden floorboards. On the dock below, a woman holding two large plastic cups filled with beer is laughing and trying to climb onto a motorboat.

"I so totally hate Florida," Vincent says after a waitress brings them the sandwiches.

"I *know*."

"Do you have any insight into why exactly Uncle Lou isn't coming? Mom gave this long, convoluted explanation about a work trip to Vancouver that was pretty clearly a lie. What gives?"

"Isn't it obvious?"

"Not to me." Vincent stirs a French fry in a blob of ketchup in his sandwich basket.

"You think he wants to watch his dead brother's wife marry someone else?"

"But it's been fifteen years! And what is a wedding without Uncle Lou anyway? He always has killer weed."

"I have complete confidence in your ability to find another source."

"Yeah, that's true." He scratches his goatee.

Katie checks the time on her phone. "Oh shit. We better

make a move. Mina will freak if we're not at the motel soon."

Mina is their older sister.

"I'm sure she's already freaking. Dude's gotta learn to chill."

"Face it, if it wasn't for her, do you think either of us would have made it here?"

"But does she have to be so . . ." Vincent searches for the right word.

"Organized? Has her shit together?" Katie stands up and pushes her chair back into place under the table. "I know, totally annoying. Now let's go!"

Katie never knew of her mother having a boyfriend or dating or anything until Dennis. It was at her mother's weekly Sunday dinner last fall when Katie first heard about him.

"Dennis is a widower too, but they never had any children," her mother was saying to Mina when Katie walked into the kitchen of her childhood home. "Her idea, not his. Says he loves kids. Biggest regret of his life." She stopped talking when she saw Katie.

"Mom has been dancing until two in the morning." Mina squeezed Katie's hand and they air kissed, the way the sisters always greeted each other. Mina was in town for her monthly business trip from New York.

"Sounds like the Red Cross is getting pretty wild," Katie said.

"Just go get the candles from the living room." Her mother's fingers mimed walking.

Katie kept listening in the hallway. Her mother never told her anything about her personal life. "So, the first night, we were setting up cot beds and Dennis says to me, we should have a race, see who can make up the first ten beds the fastest. And he won. So he says that I owe him a drink. And we went out that night and then it just kind of went on from there." Katie heard the glugging of wine being poured into glasses. "There was a group of us who went to this bar that stayed open late every night just for the volunteers. They even had a jukebox that played old songs."

Her mother dished out pot roast, mashed potatoes, and green beans, the same meal she always served for Sunday dinner, even on a humid September evening. She passed around a picture she kept in her wallet of Dennis wearing a powder-blue shirt dotted with tiny white sailboats, unbuttoned enough to reveal a deep tan. "He lives in Florida, and he says he's coming to visit." Her mother stifled a smile. "He's coming to visit *me*."

When Katie and Vincent arrive at the Shipwreck Motel, they find their older sister by the pool hunched over her laptop, holding a blue frozen drink with a matching blue umbrella in it.

Mina doesn't quite stand to say hello, just lifts herself slightly up out of her plastic lounge chair and gives them each an air kiss. "These are weirdly amazing." She indicates her drink.

"How long before we gotta leave for the wedding?" Vincent eyes the poolside bar, which is shaded and busy.

"It's not a wedding, remember? It's a party in a restaurant." Mina came down a few days early, and as usual knows more about what is going on than either of her siblings. "Dennis felt it was disrespectful to his wife's memory to have a wedding."

"So they're not getting married?" Vincent makes a face. "I don't get it. Why are we even here?"

"No dummy. They got married earlier this week at the town hall, but they wanted to have a celebration. Which is what we are going to. Which is why we are here. Which you would know all about if you ever read my emails or returned my calls or Mom's calls."

Vincent taps out a cigarette. "So how long do we have before the *party*?"

"Definitely enough time for a drink."

"Who's driving?" he asks.

They all look at each other.

"Fine, I'll do it," Mina says. "But I'm gonna be a little

pissy about it, just so you know."

"That works for me. A round of blue drinks coming up," Vincent heads for the bar.

"Why is he always like that?" Mina says once he is out of earshot.

"Are you sure about the driving?" Katie wipes the sweat off her forehead. She is still wearing her leather jacket. "Do you want me to do it?"

"Don't worry about it. You should swim. Definitely takes the edge off." Mina hands her a magnetic key. "We're up there." She points to a room on the second floor, the sliding door opened onto a tiny overhang of a balcony with lime green curtains blowing outwards.

Katie hauls the suit carrier up to their room, where her sister's clothes are all put away, her dress hanging neatly in the closet. Mina has everything that Katie doesn't, a condo, a good job with benefits, even a retirement plan. And she is the only person who will lend Katie money when she's short on her rent. Her sister spends her weekends going to college classmates' weddings, or on endless hunts for rustic-looking furniture and knick-knacks to decorate her apartment.

Katie flings her bag onto the bed, rips off her clothes and changes into a bathing suit. When she returns to the pool, Vincent is still at the bar, deep in conversation with a woman who looks like she's been there all day. When she's not talking to Vincent, she's making out with the guy seated next to her. A man in a tiny Speedo watches them and sings along to "Hotel California."

Katie jumps into the pool and tries to swim a few laps but it's hard to avoid colliding with the swirling families and flotation devices, so she gets out and joins Mina.

Katie met Dennis in a North End restaurant last fall. Her mother had just finished giving him a tour of the Boston Tea Party museum, the Freedom Trail, Paul Revere's house. He looked much the way he did in his picture and asked Katie if she was ready "to rock and roll" when the waitress came to take their order. He had a lot of questions about the entrees, talking loudly and slowly, as if the waitress didn't speak English.

"This is the first time Dennis has ever been to New England," Katie's mother said. "Can you imagine?"

"And I love it already," Dennis said.

Rose excused herself to the bathroom. Dennis chewed the ice in his drink. Katie shredded her paper napkin. Finally, her mother returned. "Well," she said as the food arrived.

"Your mother tells me you're an artist," Dennis said.

"Trying to be. I just finished school." Katie hadn't painted at all since graduation, and she'd gotten rejection letters for teaching jobs almost every week.

"I'm an art dealer of sorts." He pierced a meatball with his fork. "I sell used jewelry. And coins too. But some of my clients, they might want a painting. Or one of those things you can put on your lawn. What are they called?"

"I don't know."

"A garden gnome, that's it! Everyone has one. Probably money in that."

"I don't make those," Katie said. "I paint."

Dennis signaled for the waitress to bring them another round of drinks.

"Katie won a state championship," Rose said quickly.

"That was in high school, Mom." Katie tried to formulate a question about used coins, but couldn't think of anything, so she asked Dennis about the flight instead.

After dinner, they walked over to the harbor and Dennis wanted to take a picture of the two of them. "My girlfriend and her beautiful daughter in the moonlight," he said, the camera flashing, her mother's arm around Katie's rigid shoulders.

Vincent brings over the umbrella drinks to Katie and Mina, icy blue liquid spilling over his hands as he tries to balance them.

"Oh, that is really disgusting," Katie says after a large swallow.

"I hate . . ." Vincent starts to say.

"Jesus! We know! Stop saying that!" Katie says.

When Mina announces that it's time to get ready, they gulp down the rest of the drinks and head for their rooms. The air conditioning is on full blast and slaps Katie's skin, which has cooled down from the pool and the frozen drink.

Mina has the first shower.

"Did you know that Aunt Sylvia is having an affair," she shouts from the bathroom. "With her best friend's husband."

"Who told you that?" Katie tries to shake out the creases in her dress.

The water stops. "Mom."

"I bet she made that up."

"Yeah, probably." Mina comes out wrapped in towels, steam following her. "Hey, did you get the check I sent you?"

"I did, thanks. Sorry I forgot to tell you. I deposited it on Tuesday, I think. Oh wait, maybe it was Wednesday."

"Shower's all yours."

The bathroom sink is so low that Katie has to squat to brush her teeth. After showering, she dries herself off with a tiny, abrasive towel and changes.

"That dress is great on you." Mina looks her up and down when she emerges from the bathroom.

"Is it too wrinkly?"

"No, it's good. You look really nice." Mina smiles at her.

Katie blow-dries her hair while her sister puts on mascara, both standing in front of the blackened mirror next to the television.

"I have to tell you something," Mina says when Katie turns off the dryer.

"What is it?"

"I'm being laid off."

Katie sits down on one of the beds. "But you're the editor."

"They're being sold to another company, and they want to go in a new direction. This is my last issue."

"What? Can they do that? Like fire you like that?"

"Apparently so. Please don't tell anyone. Especially Mom." Mina puts on lipstick.

"Course I won't tell Mom." Katie leans over to buckle high-heeled shoes that will be giving her blisters in about twenty minutes. "That really sucks though."

"Well, I guess I could use a break. And I've got other offers."

Katie looks at her hands, regretting not painting her fingernails. "I'm really sorry, Mina."

"Don't be, honestly. I just needed to tell someone."

Vincent knocks at their door.

"Don't say anything to him about it," Mina whispers before he comes in.

"Your room actually smells worse than mine." Vincent is in his weddings-and-funerals attire: black jeans, white button-down shirt, skinny black tie, Doc Martens and their father's old, brown jacket with corduroy patches on the elbows that he wore every day to teach AP History at Benjamin Franklin High.

On the way to the restaurant, they don't talk. Mina focuses on the driving. Vincent balances a vodka tonic between his knees, occasionally stirring it with his finger. Katie worries about how she'll keep paying her rent, now that her sister's monthly checks are no longer an option.

Even though Katie has been working back-to-back birthday parties on the weekends, she still can't cover all her expenses. Last weekend, the birthday girl told her she was the worst clown ever. "This party is canceled," the girl shrieked, pointing at Katie who was sweating underneath her wig and her bright, red clown nose.

Right before Thanksgiving, Katie's boyfriend broke up with her, after almost a year together. He played bass and his band was constantly on the verge of signing with a major record label. They were lying in his bed when it happened. "I think we should try to slow things down," he said. At first, Katie thought he meant something sexual. But then she got it. She looked around at her clothes scattered across the floor. All she thought was how to get them on without walking around naked in front of him. "You could still come to my shows." He got up to go take a shower. Katie dressed quickly and, without saying goodbye, went home.

While she was making coffee, she got a text from Mina, telling her to call her *stat*. Katie didn't want her roommates overhearing the call, so she went onto the small back porch. It was filled with suitcases, the vacuum cleaner, newspapers and bottles intended for recycling that never made it to the sidewalk. She sat on an overturned milk crate and flipped through parenting magazines, looking for new ideas for work, and called her sister.

"What's happened?" Katie asked when her sister answered. "What's the emergency?"

"It's not an emergency. I've got big news."

"What is it then? Stop being so dramatic."

"Mom is getting married."

"To Dennis? Already?"

"Yes to Dennis. Who else?"

"I don't know. But she hardly knows him. He's going to move to Boston?"

"No, she's moving there."

"Mom is moving to Florida?" Katie's voice cracks despite her best efforts. "I saw her two days ago, and she didn't say one thing about this."

"Think she wasn't sure how you would take the news."

"Well, that's ridiculous. The whole thing is weird though, don't you think? This is like the first guy she's ever even dated since Dad, and now suddenly she's moving? And getting married? Mom could have told me. I'm thirty-two for fuck's sake."

"For one thing, Dennis is pretty old. He probably doesn't want to wait. He doesn't like living alone, and besides, they're in love. And I think Mom didn't want to tell you herself because she thought you'd be upset about her leaving, and that it might be easier if I told you."

Katie could hear a car alarm braying over and over and pictured Mina sitting out on her fire escape having a cigarette. "Are you outside?" she asked.

"I don't want to get smoke on this leather chair I got last week," Mina said.

Katie rolled her eyes.

"I heard that," her sister said. "Are you okay?"

"Yes! Why wouldn't I be?" Katie ripped out an article about shellacking leaves. Two teenage couples in the vacant lot behind Katie's building were passing around a bottle wrapped in a brown paper bag. One of them jumped on an empty soda can and the crunching sound echoed off the surrounding triple-deckers. "It would have been nice to hear it from Mom first. Anyway, who knows, maybe I'll move somewhere too."

"Maybe you will," Mina said.

The restaurant where the party is being held juts out onto an inlet, the sky blazing orange behind it.

"Okay, here we go," Vincent says once they've parked in one of the few remaining spaces.

Inside, a large bar dominates the dark, wood-paneled room which is already crowded with people. Lobster traps, buoys, and netting dangle from the ceiling. It looks like the kind of place Katie and her family used to go to at the end of a day at the beach when she was growing up. Most Saturdays in the summer were spent driving up to the North Shore. On the way home, they'd always stop at a seafood restaurant, and Katie's father insisted on sitting right next to the cover band while they ate, talking their mother into at least one dance before they left. Katie, sticky from the beach, would often fall asleep in the back seat of the car, wedged in between Vincent and Mina. When they got home, her father would have to carry her up to bed, where she'd wake up the next morning, sometimes still wearing her bathing suit.

"Do you see Mom anywhere?" Katie shouts above the band: a woman with a tin whistle, a fiddler, a guitar player, and a drummer. "How does she know so many people already?"

Vincent shrugs. "It's easier when you're old."

"Mom's not old," Mina says.

"But Dennis is," Vincent replies.

"Ugh. I really don't feel like talking to people I don't know." Katie searches for her mother amongst the clumps of seniors eating hors d'oeuvres on paper napkins.

"It will be okay. Go find Mom and I'll get drinks," Mina says.

"I'm coming with you." Vincent follows Mina.

As Katie threads her way through the crowd, she doesn't recognize a single person. She feels a rubbery hand gripping her left arm and she turns to face an older man.

"You must be one of Rose's daughters." He smiles, revealing a set of yellowing dentures that click slightly when he talks.

"Yes, I'm Katie." She shakes his hand.

"You look exactly like her. Your mother is so much fun." He grabs Katie's hands and holds onto them. "I'm Jackson. You want to dance with me?"

Before she can reply, he's leading her to the space in front of the band where other people are dancing. Holding onto her arms, he guides her across the floor in time to the music, like he's doing his own version of the waltz. A few nearby couples give Katie appreciative smiles. After two songs, she manages to extract herself from him, explaining that she needs to find her mother.

Mina and Vincent aren't at the bar. Quickly scanning the room, she can't locate anyone she knows, not even Dennis. Then she sees her mother wearing a veil, talking to Mina on the far side of the room. She heads straight for them, her high heels pinching her toes with every step.

"Oh Katie!" Her mother hugs her hard. "I can't believe you guys are really here!"

"Of course, we're here, Mom."

"Can you two help me with this stupid veil? I can't get it to stay on."

Katie and Mina follow their mother to a smaller party room in the back where everyone has left their bags. Rose sits down at one of the tables while Mina and Katie stand behind her, trying to fasten the combs in her hair.

"Ouch," she says. "You're stabbing me."

"Sorry," the sisters say at the same time.

"Do you guys think my dress too tight?" Rose asks. "I hate that look when women shove themselves into dresses that are way too small for them."

"It's perfect. You look beautiful, Mom," Mina says.

Katie nods in agreement. "You totally do, Mom."

"This is my favorite restaurant down here."

"It's really nice."

"The food here is so good. Did you guys get anything to eat?" She looks back at them.

"Not yet," Mina says. "But I'm sure we will."

"Definitely," Katie adds.

"It's been a blast since I got here. One party after another. It's so much fun. I feel like I'm in high school again. I can't believe I've only ever lived in Boston. My whole life there. I mean, it's so fun down here. Well, you'll see."

"Mom, do you have any Band-Aids? My feet are killing me," Katie says. "I hate wearing proper shoes."

Her mother searches around in her bag. "Oh shoot, such a mess in here. I know I have one somewhere."

Mina mouths to Katie when their mother isn't looking. "What's with the veil?"

"I know," Katie mouths back.

"Mom, do you need a drink or something to eat?" Mina asks.

"Oh, I would love that. I haven't eaten all day. And a glass of white wine would be absolutely perfect."

Mina heads off to get the food and wine. Her mother hands Katie a small, round bandage. "Sorry, this is all I could find."

"Thanks. That'll work."

"You should try the dolphin fish," her mother says. "It's local. And it's not really dolphin either. They just call it that."

"I'll look out for it."

"You really should. It's very tasty. Do I have anything stuck in my teeth?" Her mother curls her lips all the way back, contorting her mouth into a snarl.

"Nope. You're good to go."

"Thank you! I hate it when you've been walking around talking to people and then it turns out you've got a big blob of spinach that nobody thought to mention."

She adjusts her veil and her bra strap. "Oh, here's my Dennis," she says when he comes into the room. "Look honey.

Katie's here!"

"Katie!" He embraces her. "Now don't you look beautiful? I was wondering where my bride went. You ready to rock and roll, dear?"

"I think I am. You coming?" she says to Katie.

"I'll be right there. I need to fix my stupid feet first."

When she returns to the party, Katie leans against the wall, watching her mother move around the room, sometimes laughing so hard that she tilts her head back. Dennis is right by her side, holding her hand.

Every Sunday morning, Katie and her siblings used to get up early with their father and make pancakes so their mother could sleep in. Katie and Mina would sit on the counter, cracking eggs into a bowl, stirring the batter. They'd listen to Vincent reading the comics out loud while bluegrass played on the radio. Her father moved quickly around the kitchen, making coffee, pouring juice into glasses, setting the table, his large hands a blur above the stove top, grilling bacon and flipping pancakes. The smell of bacon and syrup would saturate the house, lingering for the rest of the day.

The band plays a slowed-down version of *Rock Around the Clock*, then *Summer Wind*. Across the room, Katie can see

Mina getting roped into a conversation with Jackson and a few other people. Katie grabs two drinks and goes to look for Vincent, but he isn't anywhere in the room, so she tries the deck. She finds him alone on a bench facing the water smoking a joint and sits next to him.

"I hate weddings," he says while inhaling.

"Figures."

Vincent passes her the joint.

"Hey listen, I gotta ask you a favor." Vincent turns to face her. "Could you lend me some money? I'll pay you back."

"I'm totally broke, I can barely pay my rent. I'm really sorry."

"No sweat. I'll hit up Mina."

He stabs out the joint and they watch the sun descend into the water.

"Did you know that when thrush migrate, they come here from like Canada and then they fly all the way to Central America in one night," he says after a while. "The whole way across the Gulf of Mexico in one go. Can you believe that shit? And they do that like twice a year. That tiny fucking bird."

"How do you even know that?"

"I was seeing this woman who was really into nature documentaries. She was like always making us watch them. And I guess some of those facts stuck with me."

"You're so weird, Vincent."

He shoves Katie slightly. A group of pelicans skim the water, and one lands on a wooden piling nearby. "You know what's good about pelicans?" Vincent lights up another joint. "Pelicans don't migrate. They fuckin' stay where they are."

They sip their drinks and watch the pelicans until it's too dark to see them anymore.

"It's kinda fucked up, isn't it?" Vincent stares at the dark water. "Both Mom's weddings we didn't see."

"Most people don't see their parents' wedding. Like ideally, you don't see your parents getting married."

"Mina sort of did."

"No, she did not."

"Mina almost did." Vincent laughs.

"There you guys are," Mina says. "I was looking everywhere for you. And *Mina almost did what*?" Their sister joins them on the bench and reaches for the joint. "Gimme some of that. You both have some nerve sneaking off to get high, leaving me in there all alone. And what did I almost do!"

"See Mom and Dad get married."

"Oh, yeah, I came pretty close to being there for it." She takes a huge hit and closes her eyes as she exhales. "I forgot why I was looking for you, shit! They're about to do the cake thing. We should go back in there."

"There is nothing I understand about this," Katie says. "It's not a wedding, but Mom is wearing a veil. And they are doing the cake thing."

"Does it matter? If you get it?" Mina says. "It's not really about us, is it?"

"It logically makes no sense."

"And there's the pot talking. Come on. Let's go. It's almost over anyway."

A crowd has gathered around Rose and Dennis. Katie and her siblings hover off to the side, watching their mother cut a piece of cake and drop it into Dennis' mouth. Everyone claps as Dennis sucks on their mother's fingers.

"Shouldn't we make a toast?" Katie whispers to Mina.

"Mom said no toasts," Mina says.

The band launches into *Can't Help Falling in Love*. Dennis and Rose dance, his hands touching the small of her back and she holds onto his shoulders, burrowing her head into his chest. Other couples join them.

One of the waitresses walks directly in front of them and Vincent stops her, as if he's ordering a drink. The next thing Katie knows, he's dancing with her, cigarette tight between his teeth.

The song merges into *Come Fly with Me,* and Vincent picks up the waitress and swings her around while she screams.

"That didn't take long," Mina whispers to Katie.

"She *is* the hottest waitress."

The waitress seems to suddenly remember that she's at work and excuses herself, but she looks flustered. Vincent dances with their mother and she laughs when he whispers something in her ear.

Dennis is walking quickly right towards Katie and Mina.

"Incoming at 11 o'clock," Katie says without opening her mouth.

But Jackson gets to them first, grabbing Katie's wrists. "Come on, sweetheart," he says and leads her towards the dance floor. She notices Mina pretending she can't hear what Dennis is saying, then point at her shoes.

After a few more songs, the band says goodnight and thank you, and the lights come on. Vincent whisks by saying he got the name of a club from the waitress, that he'll see them later, back at the motel.

"Shit, where's my sweater?" Mina looks around the room, then remembers that she left it in the bathroom and goes off to fetch it.

Katie stands with her mother while people come up to say goodbye. The sudden brightness highlights just how stoned she is. Once everyone has gone, Dennis tells her mother to meet him outside after he settles the tips. "Katie, it means the world to us that you were here tonight," he calls back over his shoulder.

Outside, the parking lot is mostly empty now, except for a cab waiting to take her mother and Dennis home.

"That was fun!" Her mother's cheeks are flushed from the wine. Her veil is loose now, the combs have started to come out, and she scrunches it back down on her head. "Oh, I had such fun. Did you have fun?"

"I did."

"Really? Did you really?"

"Really Mom. I did. It was totally nice."

"Did you meet Mary and Louise? And Jackson? You did meet Jackson, didn't you? I saw you dancing with him. That was so nice of you. To dance with him. You're coming to the . . . our house tomorrow, right?"

"Yes, Mom. I got a late flight so I can spend the day with you."

"Oh goodie. I really want to show you around. I really think you will like it."

"I'm sure I will."

Her mother reaches around in her purse, pulls out an envelope and hands it to Katie. "I was going to give this to you tomorrow. But in case you don't make it and I don't see you."

It's filled with fifty-dollar bills.

"Mom!"

"Take it, Katie. Please."

"I can't, Mom," Katie waves it away, as if it were a bug.

"I just thought . . . I didn't mean to . . ." Her mother puts the envelope back in her purse and kisses her daughter. "You'll come visit me, won't you?"

"Of course I will."

Dennis appears, grabs Katie's mother from behind and she squeals. They kiss and hug Katie goodbye, and she assures her mother that she will be at their house by ten at the very latest. Then they get into the waiting taxi and it pulls away.

Every family vacation, excursion, and day trip ended on the highway that loops around Boston, with the back seat of the station wagon folded down and Katie and her siblings sprawled on top of sleeping bags and pillows. The five of them together on their way home, shielded from the world in a cocoon of steel and rubber tires with their whole lives in front of them. As if it would always be that way.

Vincent has left with the waitress, Mina is still inside looking for her sweater. So it's only Katie waving at her mother, and then her mother's hand reaching out of the rolled-down tinted windows of the cab, until they are no longer in view. Palm fronds rustle in a warm wind. Katie clutches her elbows, her high heels crunching on top of broken seashells covering the pathway, alone outside the darkened restaurant.

The Last Supper

EVEN THOUGH IT'S ONLY THURSDAY, Jack and his family are going to watch a movie tonight, his mother announces when he gets home from school. His father is going to choose the film.

"You can have Coke to drink with dinner if you want." She mixes in a teaspoon of cold coffee into a bowl of chocolate icing. A freshly baked cake is cooling nearby on the counter.

"Even me?" Tommy asks. Their mother always tells him that five is too young for soda.

"Even you," she says.

He is so excited that he spills his apple juice. He thinks the cake and the soda with dinner and the movie on a non-weekend night are all good news.

"It's Daddy's special night. Like when it's your birthday." She's down on all fours, sponging up Tommy's drink off the linoleum floor. He nods slowly as if he understands what she's talking about.

Except it's not their father's birthday.

A month ago, Jack's mom told him and Tommy that their father got a new job, but it was so far away that he would have to move there. It would only be for a few years, she said. But she wasn't sure if they could visit him or not. Also, he was kind of nervous about his new job and they must never talk to him about it.

"Remember Tommy, when you were scared about the first day of school? Well that's how Daddy feels."

But Derek Winters, who lives across the street and used to be Jack's friend, showed everyone in the entire fourth grade the article in the paper. "Two to Five Years for Grand Larceny," the headline said.

Although Tommy couldn't read yet and never saw the news, still he was pretty confused by their mother's explanation. Tommy remembered not to ask their father anything, but he had a lot of questions for her. Where exactly was Daddy going, and what was his new job, and why couldn't they visit him? It made no sense. And he really couldn't understand why they didn't all move together, like his best friend's family did last year when his father got a job in California.

When Tommy got going with the questions, their mom would scream a tsunami of angry words and all three of them would wind up in tears. Then his mother would sit outside in the yard with a big glass of wine until it was dark and late and she forgot all about dinner. They'd eat cereal in a rush, right before bed, the milk and Honey Nut Cheerios churning around in Jack's stomach while he lay under the covers and it would take a long time to fall asleep.

Jack had to do something to make Tommy stop. He told Tommy that their dad was actually a spy on a secret mission, and if he kept asking questions, Tommy could ruin the whole thing.

"Daddy is a superhero?" Tommy asked.

"You can't tell anyone, promise?" Jack said. "And also promise that you'll stop asking Mom about his new job." So finally Tommy did.

Jack knows that tonight his father will choose *Finding Nemo*, which used to be his own favorite movie until he outgrew it. But Tommy likes it and Jack wants his dad to enjoy this evening, so he decides not to say anything. Besides, he's the big brother and part of being the big brother is sometimes you do things when you don't feel like it, his mother keeps reminding him.

Now that he's nine, Jack takes Tommy to and from the school bus stop. It's just on the next road, but he's the only one his age in the neighborhood who doesn't have a parent or some adult bringing them in the morning or meeting them later on. Sometimes the other parents whisper to each other when Jack and Tommy walk past.

"You know whose boys those are, don't you?" one of the mothers said last week. He kept his head down and told Tommy to hurry it up and stop dawdling. "I wasn't, even," Tommy whined.

Their father never eats breakfast with them anymore, stays upstairs, waiting until they've left. On the way to the school bus in the mornings, Jack glances back at the house, trying to see if maybe his father is watching them from the bedroom, ready to rush out if anything bad happens. But the light reflecting off the windows makes it hard to tell if he's there or not.

While they are finishing their after-school snack, his mother stops frosting the cake for a moment and suggests they go play in the yard so she can make sure to get everything ready in time for dinner. She looks Jack right in the eye while she talks and nods slightly. "I'll call you in when it's ready, okay."

Once they are outside, Tommy runs towards the tree house their father built for them last summer. It's made out of wood he either got at the dump or found on the beach. Tommy and Jack helped hammer the nails and attach the ladder rungs to the trunk of the large ash tree that dominates the backyard. Together, they painted it red and black, and it was their dad's idea to put glow-in-the-dark stars on the ceiling.

"For when you have sleepovers," he said.

But only one kid was allowed to come over, and that was because his family had moved recently to the neighborhood and they didn't really know anything about anybody. He turned out to be actually kind of all right and made up good games. Like pirates, the one Jack and Tommy are playing now, where they are in the tree house and there are sharks below in the grass, and they have to steal treasure from the jungle gym, which is actually a passing luxury liner. Usually Tommy likes this game and will stay in the yard until their mother lets them come back in without complaining about being hungry, or needing the bathroom, or that Jack cheated.

Now even that one kid isn't allowed to play with them anymore, and the pirate game doesn't really work with two people. When Tommy seems bored, Jack gets the rake from the side of the house and makes a big leaf pile for them to jump in. It's rained most of the week and the leaves are damp and stick to their clothes, their hair. Before they get totally wet, Jack suggests they see who can swing the highest instead. When that gets boring too, they search the edge of the yard for things that could be used for treasure like acorns and rocks and debris blown in from the storm two nights ago. They find a deflated beach ball, some plastic bags, squashed paper coffee cups. They bury them and mark the hiding spot with a pile of rocks.

They never play in front of the house anymore. Derek Winters made Jack give him the new bike he got for his birthday.

Derek Winters has a brother in high school who plays football and his friends are always in their driveway shooting hoops or out in the middle of the street playing hockey, so Jack wasn't taking any chances. He gave Derek Winters his bike and told his mom that it got stolen, although she didn't seem that interested about what happened to it. Then Jack decided that the front of the house was off-limits.

It wasn't just Derek Winters and his big brother or the swear words left in sidewalk chalk on their driveway. It was everyone.

Even Derek's mom went after them. They were in the cereal aisle at Super Stop & Shop when it happened. Tommy was hassling their mother to buy Fruity Pebbles and Jack braced himself for a full-fledged Tommy tantrum. Whenever that happened, everyone would stare at them, as if they'd never in their whole life seen some kid be an idiot in a store. His mother was explaining yet again that Fruity Pebbles were unhealthy when Mrs. Winters appeared out of nowhere, wheeling her cart straight into theirs. Jack's mother stumbled backwards from the impact and almost lost her balance.

"You got some balls going out in public! After what your husband did!" Her black raincoat hung off her shoulders like a vampire cape.

His mother's face turned pale and glassy as if she might get sick to her stomach.

"Take Tommy and wait for me by the check-out lines," she said to Jack quietly, without even moving her lips.

And for once in his life, Tommy dropped it about the Fruity Pebbles and interlocked his moist, dirty fingers with Jack's, leaning into him as they walked toward the cash registers.

Jack tried to find something funny for Tommy to look at in one of those magazines that has pictures of 400-pound babies smoking cigarettes on the cover. He could still hear Mrs. Winters shouting at their mother, who didn't seem to be saying anything at all. Tommy covered his ears, shut his eyes, and bent over, rocking slightly like he used to in his crib when he was a baby. Jack stood over him looking at the gum, feeling people's stares, as if they knew Jack and Tommy were connected to the commotion in Aisle 8.

Then boxes were toppling over and the manager was hustling Mrs. Winters out of the store.

"You're throwing me out?" She was still shouting. "She's the crook, not me!"

His mother's face was tight as she wheeled her cart toward her boys, and Jack didn't need to be told to take Tommy for a ride on the Bucking Bronco by the rows of shopping carts.

Outside the supermarket, Tommy seemed to be focusing on something off in the distance while he sat on top of the plastic white horse. Thick grey clouds lowered in the distance, announcing an imminent thunderstorm. During the drive home, they played I Spy and Jack let it go when Tommy claimed to see something with wings and called it a bald eagle, even though there weren't any.

It has been dark for almost an hour before their mother calls out into the backyard that dinner is ready. Tommy rushes ahead. Jack props the rake up against the side of the house by the hose and the garbage cans. Lights are on in the nearby houses and he can hear the din of a television, a dog barking.

Inside, his father is at the kitchen table, his face fresh and smooth, and he smells like his Gillette shaving cream. He grabs Tommy, pulls him onto his lap.

"Lemme go!" Tommy laughs and tries to squirm away, not noticing his father's grimace.

Sometimes, after Jack has gone to bed, his father comes into his room and sits on the edge and he can hear him crying. Jack lies still and pretends to be asleep, the bed moving with the weight of his father's trembling body.

His mother baked meat lasagna from scratch for a change as well as making the garlic bread herself, instead of the frozen kind that comes in plastic wrapping. The lasagna is on top of the stove, still hot, the melted cheese bubbling.

It's his mother's idea for everyone to go put on pajamas and then Tommy helps her spread out a tablecloth on the living room floor like they're on a picnic.

Jack rifles through the movies in the cupboard next to the TV until locating the *Finding Nemo* box, but the DVD isn't in it. What if it's lost? That will set his mom off. He tries the pile of loose ones scattered on the floor, then the drawers. Finally, he sees it underneath yet another stack on top of the DVD player. He puts it in, turns on the TV, and cues it up.

The food is so good, Jack has to stop himself from eating it too quickly, trying to linger on each bite to make up for all the nights they haven't had a real dinner. The plate of garlic bread is passed around and Jack decides not to look at his dad in case he is crying because that will make his stomach hurt and then he won't be able to eat. And he wonders how long it will be until his mother makes something like this again.

Jack dips the garlic bread in the tomato sauce, takes a bite of lasagna, then washes it down with Coke, piles some salad on the garlic bread. He has two more helpings, wiping up the sauce with the bread, then leans back to let the food settle.

After everyone is finished, they all move onto the couch, leaving the dirty plates and dishes of food in the middle of the floor.

"We can deal with this later," his mother whispers.

Jack sits right between his parents, his brother pressed up against his mother on the other side. Then Tommy lies down with his head in her lap and she strokes his hair and Jack wishes she would do that to him, but he's too old, or at least can't think exactly how to ask. Anyway, he's wedged tight in his dad's arms.

"Who's ready for cake?" his mother asks after a while.

"Me, me, me, me!" Tommy leaps up.

"Okay Tommy, that's enough." Even though it's dark, Jack can tell Tommy is getting on her nerves. More than anything, he wants to make it through the movie without his mother yelling and Tommy crying. Because that will definitely make his dad lose it.

"I'll help," Jack offers, hoping to divert attention away from his brother.

He follows her into the kitchen, balancing some of the dirty dishes that they leave by the sink.

"Can you get me some plates?" she asks him. "You guys want milk with this, right?"

For a second it looks like her face is going to crumple, but she catches herself and returns her attention to slicing up the cake. "I forgot how much I like this movie," she says.

She gets a tray and they put the plates of cake, milk, forks, and napkins on it. Back in the living room, Jack helps his mother pass out the cake before resuming his position tucked inside his dad's arms.

This is Jack's favorite dessert of all times, his mother's homemade chocolate cake with a cold glass of milk. He's still full from dinner but manages to get it down somehow.

When it gets to the part near the end of the movie where Nemo finds his dad, they cling to each other. Everyone is crying, even Jack.

"Come here boys," their dad says when the credits roll. They curl up in his lap and he holds them close, his arms circling them. "Get the camera, Donna, please."

While she's looking for it, Jack can feel his dad's chin on top of his head quiver. Trying to ignore his wriggling brother, he hugs his dad extra tight, taking in everything. The way his skin feels, his smell, the sound of his breathing. The lights are still off and the blue glow of the television filters out over the remains of dinner.

This moment is going to end soon after their mother comes back into the room, takes some pictures, and sends them up to bed. Jack tries to freeze it so he can come back to it at a later time. The moment when they are still like this.

Nights at the Marco Polo

IT'S THE THINGS THAT HAPPEN during the nights, inside the rooms and efficiencies at the Marco Polo Motor Lodge, that occupy Walter's days. After dark, when the traffic has eased up on the highway, there's a stillness in the lobby. The receptionists, the kitchen and housekeeping staff have all gone home, and things happen that might not occur during daylight hours. Things like adultery in Room 115, on both double beds and in the shower. Or partying in the room next door that leads to spilled drinks on the carpeting and the walls, cigarette butts swimming in partially filled plastic cups and empties, broken glass bottles, pizza slices on the ceiling. Upstairs, in 215, the aftermath of a heavy session at Odell's Tavern and possible food poisoning from the Great Wall of China takeout, the remnants on every towel and the bathmat.

Now it's morning and Walter is outside Room 115 with his fully loaded housekeeping cart. That's when he gets the call from Trish, the school secretary at his younger sister's middle school. Mallory has been at school for thirty-seven minutes. A record, even for her.

"I'm afraid we have a problem and we can't reach Mom," Trish says. It's her opening line to what has become their weekly phone call. Walter can almost hear her shaking her head, making eyes at the two other women who work in the school's front office. "We're going to have to suspend Mallory for a week. You need to come get her as soon as humanly possible. Or Mom. If she'd ever answer her phone. The thing only works if you actually turn it on."

Walter's mother works at a Family Dollar an hour away, and the manager doesn't allow cell phone use, unless she is on her midday break. But even then, Walter can't imagine that she'd ask to leave early, not for this. She'd been unemployed for a year before getting the job.

Trish explains that the school has a zero-tolerance policy when it comes to violence. "We avoid taking these measures, but I'm afraid we really had no choice here," Trish says. "Policy's pretty clear when things get physical."

"What did Mallory do?" A slight drizzle slants against Walter's cart. He's by the bank of ground-floor rooms that open directly onto the parking lot.

"Your sister broke another student's nose, Walter." Trish switches to the condescending-mixed-with-exasperated tone she uses with students.

"Was it Becky Miller's nose?" Walter asks.

Trish chokes slightly before telling Walter that she isn't at liberty to say. There would be a meeting with the guidance counselor and the principal to discuss the *incident*.

"Isn't it kind of beside the point *whose* nose Mallory broke?" Trish says. "The real point is that *Mallory* caused a physical injury on school property and the student in question was taken to the hospital. So if you or Mom could please get here, it would be much appreciated."

But if it is Becky Miller's nose, then that's exactly the point. Because Becky Miller has been torturing Mallory since the first day of sixth grade, two months ago. All because Mallory has held onto her obsession with space and doesn't care about personal hygiene. Which sets her far apart from the other girls and their obsessions with hair, clothes and who said what to whom. Not stars, planets, the galaxy, the lunar cycle, and the definitions of blue and red and blood moons.

Walter pictures Mallory crying in the school's front office amongst the gentle rumble of teachers, students, administrators, lunch aides and the security guards streaming in and out of the large sunny room on the second floor. But he still has seven turnovers and five fixes left on his roster of rooms before his shift ends, which will take hours. How long can he leave Mallory waiting there?

He puts his ear up against the door of Room 115 to see if he can hear anything, like the creaking of bedsprings. There is no sound, so he knocks hesitantly, and waits a minute. Surprising the guests at the Marco Polo is always a bad idea. He tries a couple more times before unlocking the door, readying himself for the onslaught inside. He squints into the darkness and flips on all the lights. Then he opens the curtains and windows to get rid of the stench.

Before Trish's call, the morning had started like most mornings at the Marco Polo, in the supply room readying his cart with the housekeeping staff and listening to a hard-to-believe cleaning story involving the discovery of half a finger in a bathroom sink the previous day.

"That is such bullshit." Gerri, the manager, sat at her desk, washing down a Drake's Coffee Cake with a 20-ouncer of Diet Dr. Pepper. She used to be the coach for the girls' volleyball team at the high school until she was laid off a few years back due to budget cuts. Girls' sports were the first thing on the chopping block. It doesn't take much imagination to picture Gerri shouting admonishments from the sidelines of a court. "If that's true, why am I only hearing of this now? We should call the police! Which room was it?" Gerri made like she was about to call 911. Her frosted fingernails matched the highlights of her thick, curly hair which was pulled back in a scrunchie.

The cleaner who told the story, a guy Walter knew vaguely from school, looked as if he regretted the whole endeavor and said he couldn't remember.

"Hah! I knew it. You're such a crap liar," Gerri said.

Walter and the other cleaners laughed once he was gone and finished stocking their carts with clean towels, toilet paper, individually wrapped bars of soap, and plastic cups.

"That fucking douche needs his head examined." Gerri brushed crumbs off the mound of paper covering her keyboard. "Okay, people, let's go clean some rooms!"

The Marco Polo is located out on that strip of motels where Route 1 edges the coastline. The two-lane highway starts out hopefully enough, with freshly painted motor lodges and holiday cabins lining both sides. Some even have swimming pools and advertise daily maid service or other amenities like free cable, in-room coffee, 100% refrigerated air. But slowly everything disintegrates as you get farther and farther away from the town beach. You hit the boarded-up cottages that used to be Kay's Kabins and right next door, there at the very end, is the Marco Polo. Once an actual AAA Diamond-rated motel, now it's mostly long-term renters and homeless families temporarily placed by social services. One of the rooms housed a meth lab before it was raided by the police.

But there are still enough one-night-only guests for Gerri to employ a modest-sized housekeeping staff. During his spring break from college, Walter found out that they were hiring extra cleaners to start Memorial Day Weekend for the summer season when the motel fills with back-packers looking for cheap accommodation or campers sheltering from the rain.

Despite all the build-up in his mind about college—leaving home, meeting people from different states and countries, discovering a passion—Walter's first year had been unremarkable. The classes were only slightly more interesting than his high school ones, but there was nothing he wanted to major in. He hadn't joined any clubs or tried anything new. He hated his roommate, and even more, the communal bathroom down the hall. The parties were boring, as was the small town near the campus. After a few weeks at the Marco Polo during his summer vacation, an idea began to percolate. What if he didn't go back to college?

His three younger sisters were all struggling while he'd been away. The oldest had been suspended so many times last year, she had to repeat eleventh grade. And the middle one dropped out altogether, even though she began high school on the honor roll and there was once talk of college scholarships. They both liked to point out that Walter's mother never made it through high school. They stayed out every night, sometimes getting home at dawn, and his mother had completely lost any authority over them.

And then there is Mallory. She grew so much this past summer that she's now the tallest girl in the entire sixth grade, her gangly frame hunched over. An easy target for Becky Miller, *that damn Becky Miller*, his mother always says. Mallory has become even too weird for her weird best friend, who ignores her.

Walter's mother didn't protest when he decided to take a year off, live at home, and continue working at the Marco Polo.

Clumps of wet towels and used condoms dot the floor in Room 115. Walter pulls on his yellow gloves, and although they protect the skin from germs, they do nothing to block out texture. He grabs a garbage bag and tosses in dirty plastic cups, balls of Kleenex, an empty cigarette box, peels the condoms off the rug as if they are chewing gum.

The open windows help dissipate the smell. Every room has some sort of foul odor. Even if there hasn't been a party and no one threw up. Even if it's just one person sleeping for the night and nothing else happened. The human body can't help but leave behind a trail of decay.

And when the top-dollar rooms are only $49.99 for a night, most people feel compelled to damage them, at least somewhat. Occasionally, the cleaners come upon discarded pets, and Gerri can recount all the heart attacks, drug overdoses, physical violence, the two suicides, and one attempted murder. Not infrequently, the police show up looking for crime suspects, parole violators, or runaways. Do Not Disturb signs can hang on doorknobs for days, the occupants paying cash in advance and then one day disappearing altogether.

No one knows whether or not the owners are aware of what has happened to the Marco Polo. Or if they care. They've had the motel since the 1970s but live in South Carolina now and have left the day-to-day management in Gerri's hands.

Walter has already asked Gerri several times this fall if he could leave work early to go deal with Mallory issues at school. His sister usually makes it until recess, but then there is less supervision, and Mallory has resorted to defending herself. She's pulled Becky Miller's hair, scratched her face, and last week, punched the girl in the stomach. Although Gerri is understanding, Walter is pretty sure he's used up all her good will. He'll have to clean extra fast.

Forty minutes is the maximum amount of time you are supposed to spend on a turnover room, Gerri explained after she hired Walter. In reality, it's more like twenty minutes, maybe half an hour. For the stay-overs, all that is needed is to refresh the towels, cups, soap, toilet paper, and take out the garbage. And everyone gets their room serviced, she stressed. Including the homeless families. That's the way we're doing it around here, she said, snapping her nicotine gum.

The dining area is filled with the homeless families every weekday morning, rushing to get their children fed before vans and taxis arrive to ferry them off to school. The smells of toasted English muffins and sugar cereal waft out into the reception area. The children are always scrubbed and ready to go, with their backpacks on, and they wait quietly in the lobby or talk in hushed tones to their parents or the other children. There are never scenes like mornings at Walter's house with Mallory screaming in the kitchen about how much she hates school, that she's not going, no one can make her, it's so not fair, and she hates everything and everyone. *Most especially you*, she'll shout at their mother.

Gerri complained one morning about a letter she'd received from social services that required the Marco Polo staff to keep tabs on the homeless families and report any of them who let their children play in the hallways or roam around unsupervised.

"They can kiss my ass if they think I'm gonna do that," Gerri said. "Where else are those kids supposed to go? The freakin' highway. And if any of you even think of narcing them out to some state official type person, you can go find yourself another place of employment."

Walter came across kids all the time by themselves, playing or looking after their younger siblings. Once, he cleaned a room while a girl who must have been around Mallory's age watched television and a baby slept in a car seat on the floor. The girl sat on one of the double beds eating M&M's out of a bowl, trying to use wooden chopsticks instead of her hands. Outside a heavy rain pelted at the window and it was almost cozy in there with the two of them, the Cartoon Network on, the baby blowing bubbles of spittle out of its tiny mouth with each breath. Then it had started to thunder, and the girl put her hands over her ears and whimpered. She asked Walter if he would stay with her until the storm passed. It meant he was in the room well past the forty minutes, but the storm was right above them for a long time and the girl was terrified.

Since school started, Mallory often came into Walter's room at night because of storms, bad dreams, the closet door left open, wind whipping against the house. Any unusual noise and she was charging in. "See, there it is again," she'd say. Walter would try to figure out what she meant, but he could hear only the quiet that filled the house in the middle of the night. Sometimes, she'd wake him up with urgent questions about space that couldn't wait until morning. "Why does an eclipse happen anyway?" She wanted to know last week. "Is it so everyone will stop to look up at the sky, all together, all at the same time?"

Outside the Marco Polo, cars and trucks slash through puddles as they barrel down Route 1. The scent of the nearby sea mixes with the staleness of the room as he clears off the bedside table, the desk, and the top of the TV set. A couple are fighting in the room next door, listening to Guns N' Roses at full volume.

Walter is the only one of his high school friends who moved away for college. They are still living at home and since he's been back, his social life revolves around them, doing the same things they used to do. His weekend nights are spent partying at the Thirty-Seventh Street beach, in someone's basement, or at the squatter house on Linnien Street. Except an entire year has gone by and he's missed out on all their dramas, feels out of sync with them, and some of their jokes with each other now pass him by.

Walter wipes a rag along the compressed wooden desk, the window frame. Then he washes out the ice bucket and coffee pot, refills the coffee supplies, puts a new liner in the trashcan. He sets the remote controls and Bible in their original locations, disinfects the telephone receiver and the buttons. The carpet looks much better after all the garbage has been picked up, and Walter decides he can get away without vacuuming. The Hoover barely works and takes forever to suck up the smallest amounts of dust and lint. He has to bend over to get the tube in the right position and it makes his back hurt after awhile.

Walter starts in on the double beds, taking off the dirty sheets and pillow cases and replacing them with new ones. He places a blanket on top and tucks all the bottom corners into the bed using hospital corners. Then he folds the edge of the top sheet and blanket down one inch and centers the comforter, smoothing it over the bed and covering the pillows. He pushes a small section of the comforter under the pillows, in an attempt to give it a crisp look, the way Gerri showed him.

The little extras get you the big tips, Gerri says, though Walter has yet to collect more than a few dollars from inside the tiny manila envelopes that the housekeepers leave hopefully on the desks. Often, they are empty or filled with dirty tissues, pieces of chewed gum or a few coins.

Changing the bedding makes Walter think about true crime, as if he's half-expecting to find a dead body somewhere inside the tangle of sheets and blankets. "Kidnapped Girl Found Taped Underneath Motel Bed." Walter makes up headlines as he works. "Severed Head Discovered Inside Mini-Fridge," he thinks before tackling the bathroom.

First, he turns on the shower and lets it run for a while. That usually takes care of the pubic hair. He gathers up all the dirty towels, used soap, and plastic cups. You have to fold the clean towels in this certain way, almost like napkins, before hanging them on the bars, with extra ones left on the shelf above the toilet. He sprays disinfectant cleaner on the tub, the soap holder, and the shower curtain; scrubs the toilet bowl, seat, and the outside of the toilet; wipes down the mirror, the sink, and counter; and leaves more toilet paper, tissues, cups, and soap. The last step is to mop the floor.

His cell phone vibrates in his back pocket. Trish again. He lets it go to voicemail and calls his mother even though he knows she won't pick up. After he retrieves Mallory from school, he'll take her to one of her favorite spots, the lighthouse at Windmere Point, try talking some sense into her while they look at the ocean. It's only sixth grade after all. Maybe there is enough time. Maybe she still has a chance.

"We're just a family of underachievers," his mother often claimed. But Walter doesn't want that to be their legacy. Like Mallory says, even the smaller stars still make up the galaxy, are part of a luminous body, an essential contribution to the nighttime sky.

Walter takes one last look to make sure everything is in order in Room 115. No matter what happens inside these four walls after dark, Walter will be there in the morning to vacuum, disinfect, sanitize. Erase all signs of human activity, create another blank canvas. He'll do it all over again the next day, and the one after that, and all the days and weeks and months yet to come for the foreseeable future.

A Scraping Sound of Auto Parts

YOUR SISTER IS LATE. Outside the terminal, a slight drizzle slants in the orange streetlights. Tomorrow is Thanksgiving, and everyone else from your flight has long since been picked up or connected to another destination.

You hear her car before you see it, a scraping sound of auto parts traveling across potholes. As soon as she pulls up, your thirteen-year-old nephew climbs through the passenger window and jumps on you, tries to pick you up around your knees. Your sister rushes towards you.

"Hiiieeee." She hugs your arm and then yells at your nephew to get your bag. He has pierced his left ear, a tiny silver hoop hanging off it, just like yours.

You get in on the driver's side because the other door is broken, crawl over to the passenger seat. Your nephew slides past you into the back. He bounces up and down, then shoves a CD into the stereo and turns it up loud. "This is my new favorite band," he says. Your sister adjusts the volume and asks if you're up for Thai food.

It takes a moment for her to get the engine going. "How was the trip?"

"Sucked. Baby next to me puked all over the mom. And I mean all over. Even on her face."

"Nasty." Your nephew leans across the gearshift, his head wedged between you and your sister.

"You're one to talk. You did that to me once." Your sister pushes him backwards.

"No way."

"You did, your first Christmas when we were going to Grandma and Grandpa's. Right when we got on the plane. I had to wear your dad's coat the whole way because my shirt was a total mess."

"Gross. Sorry."

"Just don't let it happen again. Baby vomit is one thing. Thirteen-year-old boy vomit is another." She stops in front of the Thai restaurant.

While she runs inside to pick up the food, your nephew turns up the music again and drums the back of your seat, the top of your head. "Your hair is almost all gone now, isn't it," he says. "You're like such an old man."

Once again, when you get to your sister's house, the first thing you notice is how clean it is. She must have gotten a gene or something that you didn't because somehow, she can work full-time, raise her son, *and* keep the house looking like this. She has candles and a tablecloth for every meal. The foil containers of food leave oily yellow stains on the batik cloth. You listen to the rest of your nephew's new favorite band while you eat. He's starting his own band, he tells you in between gulping down an entire portion of chicken curry.

Their New-Agey neighbor stops over to borrow some eggs for an apple pie she is baking. Even though she's old enough to be your mother, she has a crush on you, your sister has told you. She manages to come up with a lot of excuses to drop by whenever you are visiting. "Hey you." She gives you a long hug, patchouli wafting off her. You are only too happy when your nephew asks if you want to come up to his room and listen to some music. He plays you a song he wrote on his guitar while you sit cross-legged on the bed. The walls are covered with posters of bands and skateboarders replacing the Mariners and Sonics that were up the last time you visited.

You take out your new iPad Pro that you bought in anticipation of being hired by the television producer you met. Even if you don't get the full-time job, at the very least he'll give you an occasional rewrite or something, you told yourself. "That is so awesome," your nephew says when you show it to him. "Wanna go watch TV?"

You sit together on the living room couch while he flips through channels. Above the television, there is a framed photograph of you and him at Disneyland when he was four. You are stoned in the picture, from sharing a joint with your sister, blowing the smoke into a hit towel in the bathroom so he wouldn't notice, as if he were a parent, as if you were in high school. It was hot and you carried him around on your shoulders for most of the day. He visits you by himself now, but you still take him to amusement parks every time. It feels like being on vacation when he comes, doing all the things you wish you did more often: eating breakfast out every morning, going to the beach, hiking in the canyons.

After he goes to bed, you stay up late with your sister, sitting around the wooden table in the kitchen, drinking red wine and analyzing your older sister Nancy. She doesn't do anything except spend her days chauffeuring her twin daughters to horseback riding lessons and the tennis club in between her personal trainer workouts, buys them ridiculous presents, like matching fur coats for their eighth birthday. It is somehow satisfying saying these things out loud about Nancy, makes you both feel a little superior at two in the morning.

For Thanksgiving Dinner, you go to Ollie's, a restaurant that is similar to one you went to when you were a kid for special occasions. It seemed unbelievably fancy at the time but was basically a Denny's. Then your nephew wants to see this new skateboarding documentary. One of your friends worked on it, you start to tell him, but stop yourself. Your sister is always accusing you of name-dropping, especially in front of him. You go with him to get popcorn while she guards the seats. She told you that he has a new girlfriend and asked if you could find out more. While you wait in line, you sucker punch him in the stomach, twist his arm around.

"Stop." He smiles, lips retreating over braces. He hip-checks you and you bump into the family waiting in front.

The mother scowls. "Sorry," you say. Your nephew laughs.

"So how's the girl situation this year?" you ask him.

"What do you mean?" He turns red and looks around to see if anyone has heard.

"You know."

"I'll tell you later," he whispers. "Not here."

The three of you eat an entire vat of popcorn, your hands coated with butter and salt by the time the movie has finished.

You take a nap when you get back to their house, waking up as your nephew's friends come tumbling into the small front hallway. "That's my uncle," he says, pointing to you on the foldout couch. You wait for him to ask you up to his room, but he doesn't. His friends follow behind, looking you over as they walk by. Some have brought guitars and you can hear them through the floorboards alternating between trying to play their own songs and listening to music. He comes downstairs and asks if he can borrow your new iPad to watch a movie with his friends.

Your sister opens more wine when your parents call, and you all take turns talking to them. You stay up late drinking again with your sister, this time discussing your parents. It is not as much fun as talking about Nancy. Your sister is always angry with them for this reason or that, trying to get you on her side. There are usually long periods of time when they aren't speaking to one another. You switch to beer halfway through the evening. When your nephew's friends leave, he doesn't come downstairs to say goodnight.

In the morning, you watch more television sprawled out on the couch, your nephew curled up in the armchair. He doesn't seem interested in finding anything in particular to watch, sits there not saying much. His dad is coming to get him soon. You ask him if he's going to visit over his February vacation like he did last year. "I guess." He shrugs. "Unless I go to my dad's."

You take a shower and get changed in his room. His backpack is on the bed, stuffed with clothes and magazines. You look closer. Your iPad is in there too. Maybe he forgot that it was in his bag, you think, putting it with your things instead. You pull on your shirt and hurry out of the room, drape the towel on a hook in the bathroom.

Your sister's ex is at the kitchen table. He takes up the whole room. You were wrestling with him once years ago when they were still together, and he got you in a choke hold, wouldn't let go until your sister picked up a baseball bat. They got married when your sister was five months pregnant, divorced right after your nephew's first birthday.

"Look at you." He offers a firm right hand.

"Yeah man, how you been?" You nod slightly. Your nephew concentrates on his toast, your sister has her back to everyone, water running over dishes in the sink.

"Well we better get going." He spreads his wide hands through your nephew's hair. "Got tickets to the game," he says extra loud to make sure your sister has heard.

She turns around. "Cool." She sounds distracted, like she's busy thinking about something else. "Go get your bag, honey."

"Don't call me that! I'm not a fucking baby!"

"Don't talk to your mother like that." His father smacks him on the back of his head with an open palm. Hard. You and your sister exchange a look.

"Since when do you care?" Your nephew rushes out of the

room. Your sister starts to say something to her ex, but then seems to think better of it, and goes back to the dishes. He concentrates on the paper.

You start to follow your nephew and explain out in the hallway, away from his parents, that you took back the iPad, but it's no big deal, that you aren't worried about it or anything. Instead you just watch him leave the room. When he comes downstairs with his backpack, his face is wrinkled up. "Bye," he mumbles, not looking at you, focusing on a distant point.

"Maybe I'll see you in February, man." You do this handshake that the two of you made up when he was much younger, where you interlock elbows and make a warbling noise. He goes along with it reluctantly. Then you grab him and pull him towards you, his face cradled in your armpit.

Everyone goes out to the front of the house. Your nephew isn't wearing his earring anymore, you notice as you walk behind him. He throws his bag into the trunk of his father's car, glances back at you, gives a quick nod before sliding in, and then they drive away.

Your sister picks up some garbage on the small patch of lawn in front of the house. "Assholes," she says, crouching down over the squashed beer cans and McDonald's wrappers that someone must have thrown out of their car when they went past.

She looks especially small and young in her sweat pants and oversized T-shirt, trying to keep hold of all the garbage in her hands.

She stands there for a minute, staring at the spot where the car was, starts to go inside the house and stops, looking unsure of what to do with herself for the next twenty-four hours until her son comes back. She turns to you, as if you might have some ideas, then away, knowing you won't. When you were kids, your sister was always bringing home stray cats and dogs, injured birds, friends who were thrown out of their homes, anything or anyone she could take care of.

Her road swerves around and connects to a commercial street dotted with a Pay-O-Matic, the food warehouse, liquor stores, used furniture outlets. Your bare feet stick to the cold cement steps of the front stoop and you toe the wet strands of grass shooting up through the cracks, cradle your bare arms. Your sister takes a seat on the steps and you join her, watching the cars whoosh by. The sun slips out from underneath metallic November clouds, taking the chill out of the air before disappearing altogether.

Distant Edge of the Horizon

IT'S NEVER A GOOD SIGN when Mr. Dunn wants to do something alone with you, April's father always says. So yesterday when her father mentioned that Mr. Dunn, his boss, wanted to go fishing and would she like to come along, April should have known better. But it was early, and she wasn't fully awake. She agreed to go after he promised it would be for an hour only. "Two, tops." Her father looked into his cereal bowl while he spoke, a cocoon of silence returning to the kitchen when he finished.

They moved quietly around each other in the mornings since April's mother died in November. It was impossible not to think of her mother at breakfast. Her voice had been a constant, offering a synopsis of the news and e-mails from her sister in San Antonio, the dog clicking behind her as she moved from the refrigerator to the toaster to the silverware drawer. Now the only sounds were her father turning the pages of the newspaper or the occasional sputtering from the dog lying under the kitchen table.

April regrets her decision as she sits between her father and Mr. Dunn in his small outboard motorboat. She holds her fishing pole reluctantly, hoping nothing attaches itself to the hook dangling in the murky water below. Since the GE plant polluted the nearby river, this lake has become the most popular place to fish in the area. Modest holiday homes and cabins dot the shore, some with Jet Skis or pontoon party boats tied up to a dock. Freight trains traveling to and from Canada rattle behind the Christian family camp on the north side of the lake.

The smell of gas and algae saturate the air, and the boat lops up and down every time another one passes, making April feel queasy. Mr. Dunn suggests they try elsewhere. April checks her watch. It's been much longer than two hours, she notes. In fact, they've been out since early morning, when the water was smothered with fog so thick, you could lie on top of it. As they motored past barely visible fishing boats and canoes, the fog kept retreating, moving to some place they never quite reached, always on the distant edge of the horizon.

After they've reeled in, Mr. Dunn steers the boat towards the cove by the public beach, saying they might have better luck there. He chooses a spot that is close enough to the small stretch of sand and the roped in swimming area so that they can hear the sounds of Kiss FM from the lifeguard chair. It's been an unusually hot June and the beach is already crowded, even for a Saturday.

Once they've cast out, Mr. Dunn starts in on her father's job performance; her father tends bar during the week at the

Lantern, which Mr. Dunn owns.

"I don't understand about the karaoke. How could you not make Friday Night Karaoke a thing?" Mr. Dunn asks. "It went down like a bomb at the Parkside. In the paper and everything, it was. Everyone loves karaoke."

"But our crowd is all wrong for that. They're older and want a quiet drink after work." April's father is one of the tallest men she knows. But he doesn't look it right now, hunched over his fishing pole.

"I wonder whose fault that is!" Mr. Dunn shakes his head. "Jim, I don't know quite how to say this, but no one likes a sad bartender."

April realizes she is a decoy, her father calculating that Mr. Dunn won't go through with it, actually fire him in front of his daughter.

As they go on to argue the point, April sees her. Kyra Brody. Right there, in the middle of the raft, rocking it back and forth. Her boyfriend climbs up the ladder, grabs her around her taut, tanned stomach and throws her in. She screams and laughs at the same time. They are like a celebrity couple and the whole school follows the ups and downs of their relationship.

Kyra hoists herself up onto the raft and lies back on her fore arms. Her smooth hip bones appear at the top of her bikini bottom, and a pierced belly button glistens in the sunshine. April's hands tremble as she sneaks looks at her.

Once, when they were changing for gym class, April found herself staring at Kyra's breasts without realizing what she was doing. "Take a picture, it lasts longer," Kyra snapped at her, the only time she'd ever spoken directly to April. The memory still makes April hot with shame.

Kyra dives off the raft, surfaces, shakes her head, and swims towards the beach. Her boyfriend follows behind and they join their group of friends from April's class; she had never talked to any of them. They are the kids on the varsity sports teams, the first to start dating and smoking and shoplifting. The ones that make funny comments during class, can get everyone laughing at the shy, awkward kids like April, who are just trying to get through the day unnoticed, unscathed.

April wears hand-me-downs from her cousins and her father gives her the same jagged bowl haircut she's had since pre-K. Fashion choices that have cemented her into a social position.

After school, April always goes to the Lantern and spreads her homework out on a sticky table in a booth and the waitresses bring her mozzarella sticks, buffalo wings, nachos—snacks that usually become dinner, since she never feels like eating much when she gets home. A few customers are scattered around, too late for lunch, too early for happy hour, waiting for the after-work crowd to arrive. April's father wipes the counter with a wet rag, cuts up limes, sorts the glasses when they come steaming out of the dishwasher. Mr. Dunn is in and out of the place, talking on his cell phone, checking up on his other businesses, a water slide park and a strip club. No one ever turns off the television. When the afternoon lull is finally over and the place starts to fill, April walks home, picking up whatever groceries they need from the Quick Mart on their corner.

April's father puts down his pole. "What are you saying? People complaining about me?" He asks his boss.

"Not in so many words, but it's not a great atmosphere on the nights that you are there, if I'm being honest."

"So, what is this? You letting me go? Really? Here?"

"Come on now, don't be like that. We're just talking now aren't we. We're just having a talk."

No one says anything until there's a tug on Mr. Dunn's pole.

"Gotcha!" He reels in quickly, slapping the fish near April's feet. It thrashes around on the deck. "April, watch this."

His large hands envelop the writhing fish and he rips the hook out of its lip, bits of flesh lingering on the metal. The eyes gape as the fish begins what will eventually become its demise. Then he prepares the fish for storage in the ice chest.

April's father offers her a sandwich: homemade chicken salad that her aunt made last night. She puts in a lot of mayonnaise, celery, and a dash of paprika, the way her father likes it. He makes a small humming noise as he chews. But April is too nauseated to eat so she has a lukewarm ginger ale from the bottom of the cooler instead.

After he's finished dealing with the fish, Mr. Dunn cracks open a tallboy and winks at April. On one especially cold January afternoon, he gave April a ride home from the Lantern and made an unannounced detour, pulling into the parking lot of a single-story building. Mr. Dunn's strip club. The windows were covered with black paint and a flashing sign read "Lunch with a View."

"I need to make a little stop," he'd said. "Thirsty April?"

A woman holding a baby and a basket of clothes outside the laundromat next door stared at her as she followed Mr. Dunn inside. The place was empty except for two men seated right by a square block stage where a woman in a leopard-print thong writhed to pounding, bassline music. Mirrors behind her reflected everything not visible from the front. The walls and ceiling were covered in dark red carpet. It smelled like beer and cigar smoke.

Mr. Dunn brought April a Coke before heading for a back room. She had never seen a woman naked like this woman before. The dancer's shiny body was so tan, it was almost orange and on her chest were huge mounds of flesh high above where they should have been. Her long blonde hair was pulled back in a tight ponytail that she whipped around while rubbing herself up and down the lone pole on the stage. The two men were throwing money at her and laughing.

April didn't notice when Mr. Dunn returned until he was tapping her on the shoulder. "Hello? Anybody home?"

She startled, spilling her drink on the floor. "You enjoying the show, April?" He moved his eyebrows up and down.

When they got back into his car, there was a throbbing feeling between her legs.

A family trolling a boy in an inner tube whiz close by and the boat wallops up and down. April leans over the side and retches.

"For the love of Christ!" Mr. Dunn shouts.

Her father moves toward April and puts his hand on her back. "Oh Jeez, that's no good. Oh, April honey. You okay there?"

"Not really." April closes her eyes and throws up again.

"You two are just a bunch of laughs," Mr. Dunn says.

"I think that's it then," her father says. "I need to take April home."

"Come on, I was just kidding," Mr. Dunn says. "She'll be okay in a minute, won't she? The fish are really biting now. How about another half hour and then we'll call it a day?"

April rests her head on the edge of the boat as the vomit swirls around in the brown water. "Can you let me out?" she says to her father. "I don't mind waiting. I have a book and everything."

"Yeah? Really?" Her father chews his bottom lip, which he does whenever he's trying to make a decision. His employment could be resting on this outing. She assures him that she'll be fine and keeps her eyes closed as they putter towards the boat slip.

After they drop her off, April heads for a small grove next to the beach. She settles in on a log, pulls *The Book Thief* out of her backpack and starts to read.

April feels tired all the time, no matter how much sleep she gets. Her thoughts are like water, sliding all around in her head. The only time she can really concentrate is during science class when they dissect fetal pigs, rats, or cow eyes. Some girls triumphantly bring in notes from home saying they can't participate because of religious beliefs, but dissection is the highlight of April's week. She loves everything about it. The smell of the formaldehyde. The feel of the scalpel as it cuts through layers of flesh. The orderliness of the tiny body parts.

In the roped-in swimming area, Kyra's two best friends balance on the shoulders of some boys from April's class. One girl falls off and the boys keep dunking her head under the water. The other girl comes up behind one of them and pulls down his trunks. A boy who has already spent time in juvenile detention for arson rips off the girl's bikini top and waves it high above her head. She screams, one arm covering her chest, the other reaching for her top. The boy throws it to one of his friends and they toss it back and forth to each other, before hurling it into the reeds.

Kyra is sunning herself on the beach, rubbing oil on her legs and arms. She starts in on her stomach, not realizing her boyfriend is approaching her from behind with a bucket of water. He pours it all over her.

"Fuck you!" Kyra screams.

She scrambles to her feet and pushes him while he laughs. "It was a joke," he says.

"You're an asshole." She grabs her towel and flip flops and walks quickly towards the trees, towards April.

He reaches for her arm and misses. "Don't touch me!" she shouts.

Then he gets hold of her, pulls her towards him, but she wriggles free and smacks his face before running into the grove. "You stupid bitch," her boyfriend shouts at her. "I'm so out of here!" He gets onto his bike and pedals away, leaving a trail of dust behind him. Their friends are still wrestling with each other in the water and missed the fight altogether.

Kyra stops running when she gets near April but doesn't spot her at first. "What a fuckhead," she says to herself.

But then she sees April staring up at her. "Holy shit, I didn't know anyone else was here. What are you looking at, you fucking weirdo?"

"Nothing." April braces herself for whatever is coming next.

"You spying on me?"

"No." April stares at the ground and when she looks up again, Kyra is right over her.

"You were too. I saw you. And you were in that boat, weren't you?"

"Yeah." April's voice wavers and for a moment, she feels like she might start crying.

"Hey, relax. I'm not gonna hit you or anything. I just don't like people spying on me."

"I wasn't. I'm sorry."

"Well, which is it?" Kyra sits down next to April on the log. "Whatever, forget it." She pulls out a hairbrush, lip gloss, and eye shadow from her bag. "This day is so fucked up."

April is careful not to watch Kyra while she starts to brush her hair. "You really into fishing or something?" she asks.

"No, I hate it."

"Me too. So boring." Kyra looks at herself in her eye shadow mirror and applies lip gloss.

"And disgusting, at the same time."

"Yes, that's exactly it!" Kyra takes out a pack of Camel Lights from her bag and thumbs it open. "Want one?"

April has never held a cigarette before, but she pulls one out and Kyra lights it for her. "You know how to smoke, right?"

April shrugs.

"Inhale slowly. Like nice and easy. Like this, watch."

Kyra sucks in a small breath of smoke and holds it. "See, like that. You don't want to choke it out."

April manages to imitate her.

"Wow, look at that." Kyra smiles. "You're a total natural."

They smoke and look out over the lake. A couple of sailboats glide across the water. A large group of kayakers are landing on the beach. Several more cars pull into the parking lot and families spill out with bags and towels and sand toys. The nicotine makes April feel lightheaded. She can see her father and Mr. Dunn talking in the boat, and then they are laughing.

"Hey, your mom died, right?" Kyra asks.

April nods.

"That really sucks shit." Kyra finishes her cigarette and tosses it to the ground. "You want me to put some makeup on you?"

"Okay."

Kyra swivels around so she is straddling the log. "Here, sit like this," she says, so April does the same.

They sit facing each other and Kyra touches April's knee, poking out of her frayed, denim cut-offs. "Get closer so I can reach you." April inches towards her and Kyra leans forward, cradling April's jaw. She puts on mascara and eyeliner, her brow crinkling as she concentrates on the tiny, curled brush, the purple pencil.

"Close your eyes," she says to April.

Her soft fingertips caress April's eyelids. "Think we need to do something about your lips." Kyra strokes her chapped lips, putting on lip gloss. "And your hair could use some serious help." She runs her fingers through April's hair, tucking it behind her ears, gently brushing against her neck. April's heart pounds so loudly, she's sure Kyra can hear it.

"You look nice like that," Kyra says. "You don't have to keep your eyes closed."

When she opens them, Kyra is smiling at her. Her hands linger on the back of April's neck. She swallows, trying to keep her breathing steady. Still wet, the bikini clings to Kyra's breasts, water dripping on her stomach. Kyra is right there, inches away.

"You should definitely wear your hair back." Kyra fusses with some loose strands at the side of April's face. "Blow-dry it as soon as you get out of the shower. You know, while it's still really wet."

"Okay, I'll try that. It's not a very good haircut, is it?"

"Not really." They both laugh. "Wanna see?" Kyra lets go of April and hands her the eye shadow mirror. "See, you look so pretty when you wear makeup. How about that?"

"You're really pretty too." April looks down at her hands, her stubby, uneven fingernails.

But Kyra is busy putting everything back into her bag and doesn't seem to have heard her. "I better go. See you around, I guess." She pulls her hair back in a twist, adjusts her breasts and stands up. "Do I look okay?"

"You look excellent." April gazes up at her.

After she's gone, April gets on all fours, searching around until she finds the remains of Kyra's cigarette. Then she goes to meet her father.

"Color's back in your face," he says when they are in the car driving home. "You're feeling better?"

"Way better."

"Me too." Her father smiles a small smile. He's fixed things with Mr. Dunn, at least for now.

Later, in the quiet of evening with her father downstairs asleep in his armchair, April takes the crushed cigarette out of her pocket and lies on her bed. She has been waiting for this opportunity, like it's expensive chocolate that she is finally getting to eat. A faint hint of purple glittery lip gloss circles one end. April presses the cigarette to her open mouth. It smells of Kyra, her Hawaiian Tropic suntan oil, Herbal Essence shampoo, and tobacco, all mixed together. It smells of longing and desire and first kisses and being in love. It smells of possibility.

Inside the World of Twilight

THE SECURITY GUARD RADIOED in the code Adam, explaining to Shelley that if they couldn't find Connor, her six-year-old son, in the next ten minutes, the police would be notified. Already, the entrances and exits to the zoo had been closed, he said, and a physical description of Connor had been provided to all security and staff.

"Can you describe what he was wearing on his feet? Sneakers? Sandals?" the guard asked. Kidnappers will bring a change of clothes, he explained, but not usually shoes. He had a thick, reddish brown moustache that Shelley focused on while he spoke to her.

Only minutes ago, the worst thing about Shelley's day was dealing with her eighty-five-year old father whom she hadn't seen in ten years, and pushing him in his wheelchair in the ninety-degree heat around the zoo with Connor. Now every single person inside the World of Twilight exhibit hall, where Connor had gone missing, was staring at Shelley. She was surrounded by four guards, as she tried to recall the exact moment when she realized that her son was gone.

"Shel, what's happening?" her father barked from his wheelchair. "I have to go to the bathroom."

Her father had lung cancer which had metastasized to the point that the doctors suggested treatment would do nothing. He was too weak to walk and forgetful, but otherwise Shelley's father was exactly the same as she remembered him. Everything he did, like everything he'd ever done her entire life, enraged her, even though she rarely saw him.

"You'll regret it if you don't go visit," her older sister advised when she called to tell Shelley about the cancer. "If Connor never meets him. Trust me."

The last thing Shelley wanted to do was spend time and money flying across the country to visit her father, she argued. But her sister offered to pay for the plane tickets, so here she is. Her sister did everything for her, ever since their father left when Shelley was in kindergarten. Walked Shelley home from school, made sure she did her homework, got dinner started, gave her a bath because her mother had to work longer hours to keep the three of them afloat financially.

"I can escort him to the restroom," one of the security guards—the oldest looking of the four—said to Shelley. "Does your father need assistance?" he whispered, and Shelley shook her head no.

"Dad, this man is going to take you to the bathroom." Shelley indicated the security guard who was now holding the handles of the wheelchair.

"We don't need outsiders coming in to help," Shelley's father shouted at the guard.

"Dad." Shelley tried again. "Just go with him, okay. I'll see you in a minute. He'll bring you right back."

Once they were gone, the three remaining guards volleyed questions at Shelley. Had Connor gotten lost before? Did he like to hide? Was it possible that he thought this was a game? Was he autistic or on the spectrum? Was there anything else they should know about Connor?

But there was no explanation for his disappearance, except for something terrible had happened to her boy. Connor always stayed close to Shelley wherever they went, even in the playground. He had never run off before. He was too sensitive and shy. Most days, he cried at least once, despite Shelley's best efforts to reassure him that the world was not such a bad place and he didn't need to be so scared of everything.

But he was. He cried several times during the cross-country flight out here. At the loud roar of the engines during takeoff, when they ran into some turbulence over the Rockies, and again when they landed, bumping down onto the runway.

Connor cried when they arrived at her father's apartment after the long trip and Shelley tried to fix them a meal but found only cocktail peanuts and tonic water. She'd managed to distract him by taking him swimming in the pool at the back of the protected living complex. Throughout the visit, her father was irritable and always snapping at Connor, even though the boy was quiet and spent most of his time drawing. Shelley had lost track of how many times her father had reduced her son to tears over the past few days.

And then there was lunch in the Pink Flamingo Café, only half an hour ago. Connor had inhaled his Junior Zookeeper meal—chicken nuggets and French fries served in a sand bucket decorated with pictures of lions and zebras and elephants. Her father remarked on how much her son was eating. "See, this kid likes proper food," her father said. "Not that healthy bullcrap you insist on feeding him. No wonder he's so pale and looks like he has polio."

Connor began to dissolve. He didn't know what polio was, but he could tell that it was meant as an insult.

But her father had more to say. "The problem with you parents these days is you're so . . . you're so annoying. About everything. We never worried. All this ridiculous bullshit about not swearing in front of them and the healthy food and everything.

Treating these kids like they are fragile pieces of glass. I've got to be honest, it seems so awful the way you are going about it."

Shelley was done. "That's enough, Dad!"

"What? What'd I say?" Her father looked startled as if she had slapped him. There were crumbs covering his top lip and some ketchup on his cheek. His eyes were sunken into the puffy grey flesh surrounding them, and his cheeks slumped downwards. Hair grew out of his ears and there were liver spots on most of his flesh.

Shelley had very few childhood memories of her father. After he walked out on her mother, he would occasionally send letters to Shelley and her sister, usually containing newspaper clippings about the bands that played at the night club he managed in Los Angeles.

Shelley and her sister didn't go out to visit him until years later. A woman named Ginger picked them up at the airport, and Shelley remembered thinking she must be the same Ginger from *Gilligan's Island*. The whole day had been so surreal, flying on an airplane for the first time, getting endless sodas brought right to their seats from the flight attendants. It all seemed so glamorous.

Their mother never let them drink soda or eat sugary cereal, Wonder Bread, or any of the other foods that their friends ate. They could watch public television only, and weekends were spent being dragged to demonstrations, political meetings, and consciousness-raising events. Instead of Girl Scouts, they volunteered with Greenpeace. And her mother claimed that organized sports were part of the military industrial complex, so they went to yoga instead. This was before anyone even knew what yoga was, and before her mother became born again.

Once inside Ginger's convertible, Shelley and her sister kept smiling at each other as they rode down the Los Angeles freeway. They had never seen a woman like this Ginger except on television. The only women they knew were mothers and teachers, women who seemed perpetually tired and slightly sad. Ginger was neither. She wore a tight-fitting low-cut dress, gold hoop earrings, lots of makeup, sunglasses, and thigh-high boots. On the way to their father's house, she took the girls to a drive-thru burger place for lunch, where Shelley had her first vanilla milk shake, which was so thick she could barely suck it up through the straw. After finishing it, she had the sudden urge for the toilet, but didn't want to stop, never wanted to get out of that car. She thought she might wet herself but finally they arrived at her father's house.

Ginger showed them around and they couldn't believe it when they saw the swimming pool. No one in Jamaica Plain had a pool in their backyard, all to themselves like this one. It had a diving board and a slide, and they swam in it all afternoon. Ginger covered herself in baby oil and read magazines, occasionally getting up to bring them more soda, Doritos, and cookies. Shelley wondered if there was any way they could live there permanently.

They swam until it was dark and their father finally came home from work. They stood around the pool wrapped in thick, orange towels as he shook their hands. Shelley's fingertips were wrinkled up from being submerged in the water for so many hours.

They went out to a steak restaurant and her father got irritated when Shelley and her sister wanted to order hamburgers instead of sirloin strip like he thought they should. Then he took them to his nightclub and they both fell asleep on a pile of coats in a back office. Shelley couldn't remember much else about the trip, except for the endless afternoons by the pool and long evenings at his club. They were never invited back.

Shelley wanted to say so many things to her father right there in the Pink Flamingo Café, but what was the point? It was like sitting next to a stranger, this man who had loomed so large in her life because of his absence from it.

"Let's just get going." Shelley stood up, indicating that lunch was over.

The World of Twilight was right next door to the restaurant, and they decided to check it out. Her father asked Shelley to read the sign describing twilight which was posted by the entrance.

"'Twilight is the light from the sky between sunset and full night produced by the diffusion of sunlight through the atmosphere and its dust,'" Shelley read it loudly and slowly, so her father could understand.

"What the fuck does that mean?" her father asked.

"Dad, please watch the language." Shelley nodded her head towards Connor. It was a few more days, she reminded herself, and then they would be back home.

"Mom." Connor tugged on Shelley's sleeve. "Is twilight made out of dust?"

"This kid. This fucking kid." Her father laughed.

Connor leaned into Shelley, his face starting to scrunch up.

"Why don't we go in." Shelley struggled to maneuver the wheelchair through the heavy wooden door while holding Connor's hand at the same time.

"It's so fucking dark," her father shouted once they were inside the exhibit. "What is this?"

A few people turned to look at them, and Shelley heard someone giggling.

"Shhh. Dad. It's the World of Twilight, remember?"

"Why is it so dark? I can't see!" Her father kept shouting. "This is bullshit."

"The exhibit starts at sunset and ends at dawn," Shelley explained. "Give your eyes a minute to adjust."

She pushed the wheelchair in front of the first exhibit. It was a desert scene with wildlife that came out at sunset. Connor squealed at a rattlesnake which was pushed up right against the glass. He pointed at a mongoose, scrambling around in back.

A school trip filed in, and they were surrounded by students in uniforms with clipboards. Their teacher was shrieking at them.

"It's giving me a headache. This darkness does," Shelley's father said.

"We'll go through it quickly, okay Dad?" Shelley said.

It was then that she realized Connor's hot sticky, fingers were no longer in her hand.

"Connor," she stammered, almost whispering his name, not wanting her father to notice. "Connor honey, where are you?"

Squinting into the darkness, she searched the clumps of children huddled around the nearby cages. There he was, by the Turkish spiny mice. The band of anxiety inside her chest started to ease up as she pushed her father towards the next exhibit. But it turned out the towheaded boy was not her son.

There seemed to be small boys everywhere in the dark exhibit hall. There was a boy wearing a Padres hat. Another with a map. One holding his sister's hand, another his mother's. On his father's shoulders. Arguing with his brothers. Smacking his hands against the glass. None of these boys was her son.

"Connor!" she repeated, louder this time. "Connor!"

"What's happening?" Her father asked. "Where's the kid?"

"Dad," she bent down to speak with her father, wanting to make sure he understood her. "I'll be right back, okay. I think Connor must have gotten ahead of us."

Shelley hurried through the rest of the exhibit. She didn't see Connor anywhere. Once outside, the sudden brightness hurt her eyes as she looked over the groups of people milling around by the exit. There was another school trip, a clown selling balloons, a father shouting at his young sons, a girl screaming about a dropped ice cream cone. But no Connor anywhere amongst them.

Shelley ran around to the entrance, but he wasn't there either. She went back inside the exhibit, hoping somehow Connor would have reappeared. Her father was where Shelley had left him, shouting and cursing at a woman hovering over him. A small crowd watched the spectacle.

"Help," her father cried. "Get away from me." He was swatting at the woman, frantically waving his hands at her face. Two girls with the woman were laughing at him.

"Dad, I'm here. I'm right here," Shelley rushed to her father's side. "What's going on?"

"I was only trying to help." The woman backed away from Shelley's father. "He almost fell out of his wheelchair."

"Dad, Dad. Calm down." Shelley turned to the woman. "Thank you. I think I can take it from here."

"Where's the kid, Shel? Where is he?" her father asked.

"I don't know," Shelley admitted.

"You lost your child?" the woman said. "Oh my God. That's my worst fear. What's your child's name?"

"His name is Connor," Shelley said. "But I'm sure he's in here somewhere."

The woman was already herding the two girls towards a zoo employee by the entrance. "Connor!" The woman shouted. "Connor! Sweetheart, where are you?"

A murmur spread across the exhibit and the woman explained loudly that a child had disappeared. Soon everyone was shouting Connor's name. That's when the security guard approached Shelley, radioed in Code Adam, and Connor was officially declared missing.

Nine minutes later, when Shelley was being escorted to the administrative offices with the security guards, the call came in. Connor had been located. Somehow, he had gotten ahead of

Shelley in the darkness and ended up outside the exhibit. Then, he tried to find the entrance but got confused so he decided to wait where he was, right by the restrooms.

"Like you always told me to do if I got lost," Connor said to Shelley once they were reunited. "Wait for you to find me." And he told her the whole story over again. Which they continued to tell and re-tell throughout the rest of their visit with Shelley's father. Shelley recounted the story six months later at her father's funeral, how her father had actually been the one to spot Connor standing perfectly still outside the men's room, no more than a few hundred yards from where they were looking for him.

But some details Shelley kept to herself. Like her father telling her how calm Connor had been. "He wasn't even scared, Shel," her father said. "He knew you would find him. That you're always there for him."

And after everything settled down and new people arrived who were completely unaware of the events that had just unfolded, they resumed looking through the World of Twilight holding hands, all three of them, gripped on to one another.

"This kid, Shel," her father said as they neared the part where the sun was starting to rise, the beginning of a new day. "Some kid you got here, Shel. Some kid."

"ENGLAND IS THE BEST PLACE in the world for Christmas," Travis' father told him. But Travis had overheard his parents arguing over whose turn it was to take him for the holidays. His father had lost, agreeing reluctantly to bring him along on his business trip to the UK in late December. This will be the first time Travis has spent Christmas with his father since his parents got divorced four years ago.

They started out in Blackpool because his father was attending a convention. Travis was twelve and old enough to be on his own, his father said, while he attended meetings during the day. His father's work had something to do with website security and involved lots of traveling. In the morning, before his father left for meetings, they would look at a city map together and plot Travis' day. Blackpool's main attraction, a seaside amusement park, was already closed for the season. Most people came at this time of year because they had to for work, and it wasn't the safest place, his father said. He suggested Travis stick to the busier parts, like the promenade along the seafront. It stayed light only until mid-afternoon in December, so Travis made sure to be back in their hotel room before the sun went down. There wasn't much to see. But on the second day, Travis came upon a circus across from the promenade that was getting ready to leave town. Five female lions were being transferred from their cages into a trailer. Men stood on top of the cages, herding them with their gloved hands and wooden poles, and it seemed possible that at any moment, they'd lose control and the lions would leap out and escape.

Travis and his father also made stops in Manchester and Birmingham, but those days were filled with thrashing, horizontal rain so Travis stayed in the hotel room watching British daytime television or reading. Then they took a train down to London. His father scheduled all his meetings for the morning so he would have time in the afternoon to show Travis around. In two days, they visited everything worth seeing, his father said.

Now it's their last morning in the city, and when Travis wakes up, he finds money at the foot of his hotel bed and a note from his father, saying he'll be back in the room by 11:00 a.m. Then they'll head to Victoria station and catch a train to Brighton so his father can go to one last meeting before the Christmas holidays.

"Make sure you have a wash, Little Man," the note ends. Travis starts running a bath. There's an electric kettle on top of the mini fridge and he boils water, pours out a packet of instant coffee into a Styrofoam cup, and mixes it with powdered milk and sugar. The concoction burns the roof of his mouth and tastes awful, but he drinks the whole thing. His father says he can't even contemplate a day without coffee.

Travis studies his face for signs of hair in the bathroom mirror, but there isn't even the beginning of anything. At least his skin has remained free of acne. The small tub fills quickly, and the water gurgles into the overflow hole when he eases himself in.

Travis' parents get along well with each other, unlike many divorced parents of kids he knows. They always go out together on his birthday, just the three of them, and his father sometimes comes over for dinner, even now that his mother has a boyfriend, Dave. Since his father travels so much for work, Travis rarely stays with him, but they manage to see each other a few times a month. His parents never argue in front of him or display anything verging on anger. They seem to enjoy each other's company and Travis can't think what made them get divorced in the first place.

So, he was surprised a few weeks ago to hear his mother yelling at his father, how it wasn't fair that she had to take care of Travis so much, that his father needed to "uphold his end of the bargain." His father was dropping him home after they'd gone to a Celtics game together; a client had been able to get them second-row seats. Travis was in his bedroom with the door closed, and he was certain his parents didn't realize that he could hear everything.

His baby sister, Matilda, was born the day after Halloween, the same week that Dave moved in with them. Dave's suitcases and boxes were still in a corner of their living room. All his mother seems to do now is walk the narrow hallway of their apartment in East Cambridge, trying to stop Matilda from wailing. Or sit in the rocking chair that Dave assembled when they got home from the hospital and cry while she nurses the baby.

That day in his bedroom, Travis had heard his mother pleading with his father to take Travis with him on his trip to England. "I'm struggling here," she said. "If I could just get the baby sorted out. If you could do this one thing." And that was it, the matter was settled.

After his bath, Travis wraps a towel around his middle like his father does and looks out the window at the traffic below. Motorcycles and small cars—some with only three wheels—dart around red double-decker buses and black taxi cabs. Then he heads downstairs to the restaurant, bringing the newspaper with him.

Everyone in all the hotels they have stayed in—even if it was only for one night—would know his father's name by the time they left, the people working the reception desk coming out to say goodbye to him and Travis as if they were family. His father always makes a point to call the waitresses by their first names. After ordering a full English breakfast, Travis looks at the pictures on the front page of the paper, reads every story in the sports section, and glances at the television listings. "Thanks Rachel," he says when the waitress brings him his food. She gives him a funny look, as if he is being rude.

Travis is lying on his hotel bed watching a morning chat show when his father returns, the room quickly engulfed with the smell of his Brut After Shave. His father's face always lights up when he sees Travis, like it's been years instead of a few hours.

"Okay, Little Man. If we're quick, we could catch the 12:10." His father begins to carefully fold his shirts and trousers into a compact suitcase. He's ready before Travis has finished stuffing everything into his backpack. Cradling the phone in his neck, his father calls down to the lobby for a cab while smoothing out his shirt in the large mirror above the desk. Downstairs, the manager shakes both their hands, gives his father a discount coupon for a future visit, and they get into the waiting cab.

They drive along the Thames, past holiday work parties, everyone wearing a paper crown, and cross over Vauxhall Bridge. Gray water laps below. Victoria station is busy with holiday travelers rushing to catch trains, buying last-minute presents in the stores. People sleep wrapped in blankets near the toilets. A lone Christmas tree stands in the middle of the station. His father buys the tickets, and Travis watches the arrivals and departures board, the names of destinations and track numbers constantly changing.

Once they are on the train, his father reads the paper and Travis looks out the window as they pass through grim suburbs and meandering, brown hills dotted with sheep.

"We should call your mother when we get to the hotel," his father says right before they arrive.

As they make their way towards the station exit, the sounds of Christmas music and the beating of pigeon wings ricochet off the high ceiling. They take another cab to their hotel, but the traffic is bad, and they inch along the main road.

"At this rate, we could have walked." His father keeps checking his watch and craning his neck to see how many cars are up ahead.

When they finally reach the hotel, his father is agitated about getting to his meeting with the Southeast regional director of his company. He writes down her address on the back of a city map that he grabbed in the lobby and marks it with an *x*.

"We're having dinner there, okay Little Man? Julie lives across the street from the West Pier. You really can't miss it. It's the one that's totally falling apart. But the other pier, the Palace Pier, has got rides on it and arcades. You should check it out." He's halfway out at the door when he calls back. "We'll phone your mother later."

Travis spreads out the map on his bed. Their hotel is a couple of blocks from the Palace Pier and near the Lanes, a cluster of streets listed as one of the top attractions on the city map. Travis decides to go there first.

He meanders past stores that sell vintage clothing, used books, antique jewelry, and local artists' paintings and crafts. The cobblestone streets are crowded with holiday shoppers. He passes a children's clothing store and decides to get something for his baby sister.

Every afternoon since the baby was born when Travis got home from school, his mother would still be in her sweatpants and T-shirt, the same thing she was wearing in the morning. And she has gotten infections three times already, because the baby has trouble "latching on," he has heard her telling her friends on the phone. The baby is not gaining enough, and they keep having to go to the doctor to get her weighed.

Right before Matilda was born, Travis was in a school play for the first time. His mother helped him rehearse his part, figuring out how many lines he needed to memorize each day. But the night of the performance, the doctor said she needed to stay in bed, so Dave recorded the play for her. Afterwards, when they got home, they all crowded together on his mother's bed to watch Travis' performance. The recording mostly showed the tops of people's heads in the audience and you could barely see the stage, but his mother said she could still tell he had a real talent.

Travis looks through the onesies and baby shoes. But he has only seven pounds left, so he buys a plastic crab rattle instead. He asks the woman behind the counter to wrap it up for him, and chooses a purple ribbon, his mother's favorite color. Clutching the present, he walks down to the pier that sticks out from the stony beach. "Palace Pier," a huge arch announces in red light bulbs. Farther down the beach, Travis can just about make out the other, decrepit pier as daylight fades. The Southeast regional director's house must be right across the street.

Travis walks the length of the pier past the arcades with food stalls selling fish and chips, burgers, ice creams. Past the fun fair rides, the carousel with its dragons going around in circles, and out to the roller coaster at the end. On the way back, he cuts through the arcade, busy with teenagers and children. A group of older men are trying to win a stuffed animal, pounding on the claw machine each time they fail.

Next door to the arcade is a pub, and Travis follows a couple in. Cigarette smoke hangs from the ceiling like fog. There is no music playing, only the murmur of conversations from the few people scattered around the small tables. Travis orders a Coke from the bartender who informs him that he'll need to leave when it gets busier. Travis hands over the last of his change and takes a seat at a table near the door.

He has always liked the smell of bars, the mixture of smoke and stale beer, and this pub is no different. When he was younger, his mother used to bring him along on dates if she couldn't find someone to look after him. Travis would sit in a cocktail lounge, doing a word game book in the corner of the booth, while his mother laughed at different men's jokes.

He was used to being quiet around other people, especially adults. The evenings with his father had been spent attending client dinners, with Travis reading or drawing cartoons. Travis thought of it as his secret superpower, this ability to become almost completely silent and still, as if he had disappeared altogether. He even made up a comic based on the sensation called Invisible-Visible Guy who can fight crime and save people while his body remains at his desk or in a restaurant, with no one around him realizing he has gone.

Travis lingers over his soda until the bartender comes over. "You better get going now, son." He snatches the glass away from the table.

It is dark now, and he walks along the sea front until he reaches the old pier. Yellow police tape blocks the entrance and a sign says "Danger—Keep Off." He looks at the gaping holes in the walkway that connects a dilapidated building to a pavilion out on the tip. Then he crosses over the main road.

He rings the bell at the regional director's house and waits for someone to let him in. A tall woman opens the door, wearing a tight black dress that is so low-cut he can see everything. "You must be Travis," she says. "I'm Julie." She is much younger than he imagined a regional director would be.

"Hey Little Man," his father calls from the leather sofa in the living room. As Travis gets closer, he can see a dent next to him where Julie must have been. Their Christmas tree smothered in lights stands by sliding glass doors that open out onto a deck. "Did you have a good afternoon?" His father's shirt is pulled out of his trousers.

Travis nods and turns away while his father tucks it back in.

"So, this is Travis?" Julie smiles at his father.

"The very one."

"Well, I am very pleased to meet you. Right, now let me see if I can get my monsters down here." Julie stands at the bottom of the staircase, calling with increasing urgency. Finally, there is the sound of pounding footsteps above them, then on the stairs and two boys appear, one slightly larger than the other.

Julie introduces "my twin monsters" and their names, but Travis forgets which one is which. They appear to be about his age. The larger one has his head completely shaved and offers a handshake. The smaller one's face is barely visible beneath a pulled down baseball cap without a team logo on it. He makes a snarling noise at Travis.

"Behave," Julie warns and suggests they eat. The dining room table by the Christmas tree has already been set and Julie directs everyone to their chairs. She hurries in and out of the kitchen, serving platters of overdone beef and boiled, flavorless vegetables. But Travis is so hungry he manages to get it all down.

The twins snicker at each other while Travis' father tries to get a conversation going. First, he tries English football, but that doesn't go over well.

"Don't even mention Man United in this house, right?" The smaller one pounds the table with his fist.

"That's enough!" His mother says.

"But Mum, seriously?"

"I don't have an opinion on them," his father says. "I've just heard of them. Guess we better move onto a more neutral topic."

He winks at Travis when the twins aren't looking, and the rest of the meal is without conversation. As soon as they are finished, Julie gets the larger twin to clear while she offers dessert. The twins balk when they hear it's an apple crumble.

"Why do we always have crap pudding when Mr. Turd is here?" The smaller one lifts his head slightly so the lower half of his face is visible.

"You know very well that his name is Mr. Heard. And if you want something else, why don't you take Travis to go get ice cream on the pier? I'll give you some money for games as well. And there's going to be fireworks later."

The twins whine at the suggestion, but they go get their coats before Travis gets a chance to say that he's already seen the pier and would prefer to stay here.

"Hey, have fun, okay?" his father winks at him again.

It's raining lightly, like someone is spraying them with a plant mister. The twins walk quickly past the falling-down pier, and Travis has to almost run to keep up with them. When they get closer to the Palace Pier, the walkway becomes increasingly crowded and Travis struggles not to lose sight of the twins altogether.

They stop at the arcade and the twins head for the only vacant game that has guns. Travis finds a pinball machine and plays a few rounds by himself before wandering outside to look at the ocean. The green swelling waves pound the wooden pilings below and he looks out over the water for a while before going back inside to find the twins.

They are about to leave. "We have to be somewhere," the larger one says. They seem annoyed that he has found them and talk about him as if he wasn't there.

"Mr. Turd's son is a big giant turd, like Mr. Turd." The smaller one snorts.

Once again, they rush ahead, looking back occasionally at Travis, say something to each other before laughing. They thread their way through side streets set back from the beach. No one else is around. Then they stop and turn to face Travis, and it seems like they might hit him.

"So, when's your stupid dad moving here then?" the small one asks.

"What?"

"Don't pretend like you don't know about it," the small one says. "We heard Mum telling her friend that your dad is moving in with us. But when we asked her, she said they were just talking about it, and it wasn't for definite or anything."

"But we can tell she's lying," the larger one adds.

"So, when's it happening?" the smaller one asks.

Travis feels as if all the air is being sucked out of him. "I don't know," he mumbles.

"Don't fuck with us, alright?" the small one says. "Course you know. Fucking tell us, you wanker." He steps closer to Travis, but the larger one pulls him away.

"Leave it. Come on then, Sophie's waiting for us." The larger one says, and they continue on their way toward wherever it is they are going.

But Travis slows his pace, no longer caring about being left behind. In fact, he'd prefer to go back to the hotel and be alone, so he can digest this new information, that his father is moving to England. But before long, the twins stop in front of an attached house with a red door. "Hurry it up, will you?" the smaller one shouts back at him. "We're here."

Travis catches up with them and waits on the sidewalk, and the twins knock on the door. After a few minutes, a girl pops her head out. "Who's that then?" she asks the twins, indicating Travis, hovering by the bushes that bookmark the entranceway to the girl's house.

"Mr. Turd's son. We had to bring him," the smaller twin says. "He's American too, same as Mr. Turd."

"Your mum likes American blokes, doesn't she?" The girl has red hair and she gives Travis a once-over. "You coming in or what?"

Travis shrugs and follows the twins inside. He has no idea where he is, and at this point, it seems easier to stay with them. The girl leads them down a hallway to her bedroom which is covered with posters of bands Travis doesn't recognize. The larger twin sits on the bed next to the girl, Travis and the smaller twin on the floor. No one takes his coat off.

The girl pulls a bottle of Wild Turkey from under her bed and passes it around. They all take quick swigs, and she puts on a CD of The Cure on her boom box and turns up the volume. Then the larger twin starts kissing her.

On top of the girl's bookshelf, there is a picture of her with two girls dressed in miniskirts, singing into a microphone. She is the prettiest girl in the picture, and Travis realizes that she might be the prettiest girl he has ever seen.

"That's enough then," the girl says and pushes the larger twin onto the floor. "You can have a turn if you want to," she says to Travis. One of his legs has fallen asleep and he stumbles slightly when he stands up. The twins laugh at him.

"Shut up," the girl says.

Travis sits next to her on the bed, and takes off his jacket, while the girl watches him. She passes him the bottle; he takes a drink and gives it back to her. The Wild Turkey makes him feel warm and loose. The girl moves right next to Travis, raises her mouth up to his, and kisses him.

Travis has kissed only one other girl before, this past summer on the last night of sleepover camp, two rushed minutes behind an outhouse. He tries to concentrate on the girl's lips, and then suddenly her tongue is in his mouth, wrapping around his, sliding along his teeth. She slowly leans him back onto her pillows.

"Sophie, he's having too long," the smaller twin says.

"Get out!" Sophie shouts at them. "Now!"

When they've gone, she lies on top of Travis, pressing into his groin, her hand reaching up his shirt. He doesn't know how long they have been kissing when she offers to take her shirt off. "I've never kissed an American before." She sits up, pulling her T-shirt over her head, and unsnaps her bra.

He has never seen breasts up close, and he timidly touches them, and then she is back on top of him. Her lips lead his, her body slowly grinding into him. This seems to go on for a while before they are interrupted by pounding on her bedroom door.

"Sophie! We have to meet Dad for the fireworks," her brother shouts. "Let's go!"

She pulls away from Travis. "Fucking hell," she says, rolling off him, reaching for her shirt. He lies there watching her dress and quickly brush her hair. "Get a move on, would you," she smiles at him. "We have to go."

Travis feels like he is going to fall over when he stands up, his legs rubbery and unstable. But he manages to get it together and follow Sophie down the hallway where the twins and her brother are waiting. Sophie's brother towers over them, a long scar dominates his left cheek. "You lovebirds ready?" he says.

"Shut up," Sophie says.

It is raining now, a hard, steady rain, and Travis keeps his head tucked down as they head towards the main road. It is a steep downhill and as they get closer to the center of town, it gets busier and busier. When they have almost reached the main road that runs parallel to the beach, they struggle to stay together. Some people are even running, and Travis can hear sirens in the distance. Sophie's brother asks an elderly couple what's happening.

"The old pier has collapsed," the man says.

"I always said that pier would fall down," his companion's face tightens underneath a scarf tied around her head.

"You absolutely did not," the man snaps at her. "Don't talk such rubbish."

They wait for the light to change before going over to the seafront. Two boys holding their mother's hands complain that it's too far and too cold. A group of girls skip arm in arm, singing the same pop song Travis has heard everywhere he's been in England. Sophie's brother and the twins start singing English football songs, and soon other people join in.

The beach is swarming with people in raincoats collecting pieces of wood from the pier that have already washed ashore. Two police boats surround the old pier, their lights illuminating the crumpled structure. The middle walkway is completely gone, and half of the main building hangs down over the water at a sharp angle, threatening to slide away at any moment. Teenagers jostle in tight circles and children are running around, throwing rocks into the waves.

Sophie's brother sees his friends off in the distance, tells Sophie to meet him and their dad in ten minutes. "That same place where we watched the fireworks last year, remember, Soph?"

The larger twin kicks at the pebbles on the beach, his hands shoved in his pockets. "This is pathetic," the smaller one says to his brother. "Just a bunch of wood. I'm hungry. Let's go get burgers."

When they've gone, Sophie grabs Travis' hand and they walk to the edge of the water. Someone starts to swim out towards the pier, but he doesn't get very far before turning around. More police are along the beach, monitoring the growing crowd. There's even a small news crew.

"What's your name?" Sophie turns towards Travis. They are both completely soaked.

"Travis," he says. Sophie smiles as the rain pelts her upturned face. She grabs both his hands and puts them inside her coat pockets, pulling him closer.

Behind Sophie, Travis can see Julie's house. All the lights are out, except for the ones on the Christmas tree, blinking off and on.

He wants to point it out to Sophie, his father's new home. Travis thought they would spend Christmas together, just the two of them, in their hotel room, but now he's not so sure. They'll fly home on Boxing Day and when they land at Logan, his father will be rushing to catch a connecting flight for another city and more meetings, so they will say goodbye at the gate. He already told Travis that he has so many business trips in the coming months, they probably won't see each other again until Easter. A flight attendant will bring him out to Dave, waiting in baggage claim. The streets will be dark and empty when they drive home to his mother in her sweatpants, consumed with taking care of the baby.

Travis wishes he could tell Sophie how his parents have broken away from each other and are now moving on with their new families, and Travis is on the outer edges of it all. But there are only a few more minutes before Sophie has to leave, so Travis doesn't say anything. Besides, she has her head resting on his shoulder, her warm breath on his neck, and for now it is enough to have this small, good feeling of being pressed against a pretty girl on a wet winter evening.

We Were Lucky with the Rain

LACEY CAN'T RESIST SPYING on her parents when they fight. Which happens whenever her mother has disappeared for a few hours or, occasionally, the entire evening. Lacey lies flat on the wooden floor of their upstairs hallway, peering through the banister at her parents, who are yelling at each other in the living room below.

Her father wants to know where her mother has been and why she never picked up Lacey from her piano lesson this afternoon, or her younger sister, Eileen, after school.

"I told you this morning that I was going to this Mom lunch thing at Hoolihan's. So I was late, okay?" Lacey's mother throws her purse onto the floor. Only her legs are visible underneath a red dress, as she roams around the living room. She bumps into the coffee table, left ankle buckling.

"You weren't late, you didn't show up. You didn't answer your phone. We had no idea where you were. And now you're a complete mess." Her father's voice goes up an octave. "You could have killed someone, you know."

Her mother starts laughing. "Jesus, relax. I took a cab."

"Then where is the car, goddamn it?"

If Lacey tilts her head a certain way, she can see her father's slippers pacing back and forth. She strokes her fraying rope bracelet that she got at her school's Fall Festival. Her fingers always work their way to its soft underside whenever she's waiting for her turn to bat for her softball team or perform in a piano recital.

"The car is fine, all right?" her mother says. "I left it in the parking lot at that Star Market by Hoolihan's."

"It's not *fine*. It won't be *fine*. You can't leave the car there overnight. It's going to get towed!" Her father's slippers stop moving. Then he stomps his left foot on the floor and throws a sofa cushion out into the hallway. A table lamp crashes to the floor and her mother shouts at him to *Stop it, just stop it.*

Lacey can't understand how Eileen always sleeps through their parents' arguments, which often involve things being broken. A few weeks ago, her mother hurled a bottle of red wine against the front door. Another time it was plates. She's also thrown glasses, shoes, and once a dining room chair. But her father always cleans it all up, and in the morning, there is never a trace of the mess, not even one thing out of place anywhere.

Every Friday, Lacey's mother picks her up after her piano lesson at 4:30. But this afternoon, 4:30 came and went, then it was 5:00. Lacey waited for her mother through the next lesson, and the one after that. Her mother never came.

Lacey sat out in the hallway on a bench, her back pressed up against the wall. The lessons were in the living room and Lacey could hear the metronome and Mrs. Szabo counting, "One and two and one and two," fumbling scales going up and down the piano. The hallway's striped yellow wallpaper was covered with faded photographs. It smelled of old furniture and rugs, mold and dust, like Lacey's basement. She pulled out her notebook to work on a sketch of the teacher she'd started during marth class. He wore suits with purple basketball sneakers and was known for throwing chalk at anyone not listening.

"Still no mother?" Mrs. Szabo said when all the lessons were finished for the day and then asking if Lacey wanted to call her. Her mother's phone went straight to voice mail, so Lacey returned to the hallway bench while her teacher started dinner. The black baby grand was shoved in a corner of the living room. During the lessons, Mrs. Szabo always sat next to Lacey on a folding chair, making sure that her hands didn't slouch onto the keys, that she sat up straight, back like a board, shoulders down. Lacey hadn't practiced very much during the week—one piece she didn't work on at all—and Mrs. Szabo was annoyed with her. "You're not trying. Put some porridge into your playing," she'd said, wiping her nose on the ball of Kleenex that was always tucked inside her sweater. There was going to be a recital in three weeks and Lacey wasn't close to being ready. Usually she received stars on all her pieces, but this week she got none.

By the time Mr. Szabo got home, the hallway had become a mixture of smells, sautéing garlic, grilled chicken, and damp basement. Lacey could hear them discussing her in the kitchen, sometimes slipping into another language. "They're survivors, honey," Lacey's mother would say in a hushed voice whenever Eileen wanted to know why they "talked so funny."

"Mister will give you a ride home," Mrs. Szabo came out to the hallway. "You must practice an extra half hour each day this week."

As he drove, Mr. Szabo leaned way over the steering wheel and waited a long time at intersections to make sure nothing was coming. Cars honked at every traffic light, and Lacey hoped they wouldn't see anyone from school. "Missus tells me you are a good piano player," he said when they finally arrived at her house.

Lacey let herself in through the kitchen door and went through the dark house turning on all the lights downstairs. She sat in the window seat of their breakfast nook and pulled out her notebook and finished the sketch of her math teacher. The stove clock flipped over numbers and an occasional car drove by.

After a while, her father's Jeep Cherokee turned into the driveway, Neil Young blasting out of the open windows. When Lacey's father came through the door, he was singing to himself, but stopped abruptly at the sight of Lacey alone and the absence of dinner.

"Where's Mom?" He pushed his glasses back onto the bridge of his nose.

"Dunno."

"Didn't you have your piano lesson today?"

Lacey nodded.

"Did your mother pick you up?"

Lacey shook her head. He stood in the middle of the kitchen, running his hands through his starting-to-gray curly hair, which could never seem to find a comfortable place on his head. "What about Eileen?" he asked. "She's not home either?"

"Nope." Lacey was starving, but her father would be distracted trying to find Eileen and her mother. Dinner wasn't going to happen as usual when Lacey's mother disappeared.

Her father took a seat at the kitchen table and started calling around the families they knew from school and various neighbors. Lacey went upstairs and ate some crackers and cookies stolen from the kitchen that were stashed away in the bottom drawer of her bureau. But they only left a hollow, empty feeling in her stomach. Then she dove onto her bed and looked out the window.

Lacey had chosen the smaller bedroom when they moved here five years ago because it faced the street. There was a clear view into the homes directly opposite Lacey's, and she could monitor all sidewalk activity as well. Usually there wasn't much of interest to observe in the evenings, just the neighbors coming home from work or taking out the trash or walking their dogs.

A car pulled up in front of their house and Eileen shot from the back and ran towards her father who shouted "Thank you" as he stood in the kitchen doorway. Lacey lay down and studied the water stains on the ceiling. Eileen came bounding up the stairs, before bursting into Lacey's room.

"Mom is in so much trouble," Eileen panted. "Dad says he has no idea where she is." Eileen's hair was in loose braids, leftover from yesterday.

"She can't be in trouble, she's Mom, you idiot." Lacey rolled over onto her stomach and stared at her sister.

"I had to go home with Tracy, and she smells weird, and then I had to eat dinner with them, and everything was green." She stood in the middle of the doorframe, pressing her hands against it. "I think I'm going to barf."

Lacey yawned and covered her ears.

"Why are you *so* mean?"

As a reply, Lacey started humming loudly.

"I. Hate. YOU!"

"Eileen, it's time for bed," Lacey's father called up.

Eileen went out to the hallway to complain that it wasn't fair she had to go to bed earlier than Lacey. Then there were the sounds of water running in the bathroom, and her sister's bedroom door slamming. Lacey pulled *Roll of Thunder, Hear My Cry* out of her backpack and started reading, glancing out the window after every paragraph.

When she had finished the two chapters she was supposed to read for homework, a taxi stopped in front of the house. Her mother got out and started walking slowly towards the front door, steadying herself as if she were on a boat. Lacey scurried over to the staircase, trying not to make any noise on the wooden floorboards. Downstairs, her father sat in the orange armchair which was stuck in the recline position, parked between the front bay of windows and the TV, reading the newspaper. As soon as her mother opened the door, he stood up.

Breath mints spill out of her mother's purse when it hits the floor and roll around. Her mother never wears red dresses to hang out with her "mom" friends or when she picks up Lacey and her sister in the afternoons from their various activities before doing the errands.

Her mother hates errands, especially going to the supermarket. She usually gives Lacey and Eileen the grocery list and waits in the checkout line reading magazines. They each grab a cart and split up the list, racing each other around the store. Their mother buys them a candy bar after they've finished. "My helper girls," she says while they bag the groceries. But the best part is walking down all the aisles looking at the variety of pasta, sauces, salad dressing, spices, each item containing the promise of some perfect meal. Whenever Lacey goes to the next-door neighbors' house for dinner, they usually have company, kids from school, cousins, family friends from other countries. Everyone crowds into the kitchen to help make dinner. There are always fresh vegetables and herbs, pre-soaked beans, and nothing comes out of a can.

Her father wheels the bike out from the side of the house and sets off to retrieve the car. Lacey gets back in bed and starts reading again. She can hear her mother on the stairs.

"Can I come in?" Her mother is in Lacey's doorway and she takes off her high heels. Lacey doesn't look up from her book. She crosses the room and sits at the end of the bed.

"I'm sorry I didn't pick you up from your piano lesson

today," she says. Lacey keeps reading. "Sometimes I get carried away." The same excuse she always uses to explain her absences.

After finishing the next chapter, Lacey turns off the light and pulls the blankets tightly around herself. Her mother keeps sitting there in the dark looking at her. "You were such a good baby." She smooths the covers over Lacey, her hand resting on her daughter's shoulders. When she was younger, Lacey could only fall asleep if her mother tickled her back. She strokes Lacey's hair, then gets up and walks quietly out of the room, closing the door behind her.

In the morning, Lacey goes down to the kitchen where her father and Eileen are having breakfast. Usually her father is barricaded behind the paper, but today he is staring ahead at nothing in particular. Eileen is eating Pop-Tarts, which they are allowed only on special occasions like Christmas or school vacations, but their father doesn't know any better. Lacey warms one up in the toaster, spreads butter on it. She sits across from Eileen, letting each bite linger on her tongue for a minute before chewing.

Her father finishes his coffee and then starts unloading the dishwasher. "I almost forgot. It's Road Trip Day," he says.

"Do I have to go?" Lacey asks.

There is nothing she hates more than Road Trip Day. Ever since she can remember, her father has designated the first Saturday of the month for family outings that are never fun. He takes them to flea markets in other states, obscure historical landmarks, or on long, destinationless hikes. And they wind up getting lost because he gets sidetracked by garden stores and garage sales, buying knickknacks and broken furniture that their mother ends up throwing out months later. Lacey's mother has long since stopped coming on these excursions, has "Mom alone time" whenever they go off in search of whatever her father is looking for.

"Just go get dressed," he snaps at her.

Lacey looks at Eileen who is oblivious to everything before shuffling upstairs to take a shower. While she is getting dressed, Eileen comes into her bedroom.

"Why are you so mean to Dad?"

"I'm not mean," Lacey says.

"You are. You're mean to everyone. Especially me. And I didn't even do anything." Her sister swallows a few times like she does when she is trying not to cry.

"You want me to braid your hair?" Lacey switches to her gentle voice.

"Okay." Eileen sits on the floor by the bed and Lacey combs her sister's hair, separating it into three sections, then weaving them together.

When they were younger, they used to dress up in their mother's clothes, high heels and boots, and her jewelry. They'd fish out necklaces and bracelets from their mother's blue, wooden box that was next to a picture of their brother who died when he was three months old. Eileen wasn't born yet, and Lacey was only two when it happened, and she probably wouldn't remember him, except for the tiny picture in the silver frame on the bureau.

Downstairs, her father waits for them in the orange chair thumbing through his well-worn guidebook which runs the gamut from information about national parks and monuments to the World's Largest Ball of String and Car-Henge, a replica of Stonehenge. "There's an alligator farm about an hour away from here." He doesn't look up from the book. "It sounds great. And we could hit the outlets on the way home."

By the time they are ready to leave, there is still no sign of Lacey's mother, except for the sound of the toilet flushing in the bathroom upstairs while they were having breakfast. Early morning dew still covers the ground and it smells like fresh-cut grass. Next door, the driveway is already empty. The entire family has already headed off for the day. The whole neighborhood is always in their backyard, the kitchen, or their basement rec room.

Lacey crouches down when they turn off their street and head onto Woodbine Ave. Osco Drug is right on the corner where kids go after school to steal candy bars, skateboard in the parking lot, maybe even smoke a cigarette. But fortunately, no one is there right now.

Eileen insisted on sitting in the front seat so she could be in charge of the music. But she keeps changing radio stations, and finally their father puts on his Neil Young CD despite Eileen's protests.

It starts to rain. Lacey looks out the window as they hurtle past the Burlington Mall, the Woburn Mall, a state liquor store, discount furniture warehouse. Gradually the landscape gives way to trees, hills even an occasional farm as they head farther and farther into the countryside.

It takes nearly two hours to get to the alligator farm. Lacey feels slightly carsick by the time they arrive, but the rain has subsided. The visitors' parking lot is empty.

Lacey's father rushes up to the entrance booth, shouting out "Well, hello there" to the man sitting behind the desk. He is wearing a brown woolen hat and takes the money without saying anything, shoves a brochure and change back through the slot in the plastic window.

Lacey and Eileen dodge puddles, trying to keep up with their father. "Girls, come look at this." He indicates a hissing bobcat, taking up almost the entire cage. "Isn't that something?" There are no signs on any of the small, filthy cages, just a soggy animal penned in behind wire mesh that smells like an outhouse with barely enough room to turn around, gnawed chicken bones in the corner. One cage contains a molting owl, another, two foxes, and at the end, there is a panther. They are still the only ones in the whole place, which looks temporary, like a summer fairground that could be packed up in an hour before moving on to the next town. Another great choice by her father.

Then they come upon the alligator pits, five concrete fenced-in areas. Each one has a watering hole, a trough, and a pile of hay in a corner, and looks better suited for a pig.

"You know the difference between a crocodile and an alligator?" Their father reads from the brochure. Eileen and Lacey make faces at each other. "It says here that alligators have wider U-shaped snouts, and they prefer freshwater marshes and lakes, while crocodiles mostly live in saltwater habitats and their snouts are shorter and they look like they are smiling."

Lacey looks at her watch and tries to calculate how many more minutes it will be until this is over.

They watch an alligator walk towards the water and slide itself in.

"This is gross," Eileen says. "I'm hungry."

"Let's go have a look at the other ones." Their father steers them towards the rest of the alligators. One has duct tape wrapped around a foot. Another is missing an eye.

"Daaaddy? I'm hungry," Eileen whines again.

"Okay, okay. I heard you." He fishes around in his backpack and pulls out the camera. "I want to get a picture of you girls for your mom first. She's going to be sorry she missed this."

They stand next to each other, waiting while their father focuses the camera. It starts to rain again, much harder this time. They head for cover, an overhang near the panther, and crowd together, trying to stay dry.

"We better run for it," their father says.

Their shoes squelch as they hurry back past all the cages. By the time they reach the parking lot, their car is still the only one there. Lacey claims the front seat before Eileen can get to it, but she doesn't say anything and slides into the back.

"Wasn't that great, girls?" Lacey's father dries his glasses off with the inside of his shirt.

"It was totally gross, Daddy." Eileen says. Lacey takes off her wet shoes and socks, her toes are red with cold.

"It was *totally* interesting." He reaches for the glove compartment and pulls out his diner guidebook. "There's supposed to be a great pancake place near here."

"I'm not even hungry anymore. I think I'm going to barf." Eileen shakes out her wet hair before lying down along the back seat.

Lacey's father decides on a different route home that will take them through a mountain range before the pancake restaurant. Rain pelts the car as the windshield wipers flap back and forth. Lacey closes her eyes and rests her head against the window, her cheek sticking slightly to the cool glass. Hot, thick air blasts in from the vents on the dashboard. She has trouble remembering her mother coming on these trips. Was she there when they went to Old Sturbridge Village? Or the Shaker museum? The last time Lacey can definitely picture her being with them was when they went to the whaling museum in New Bedford, but that must have been at least two years ago.

It is raining so hard now, Lacey can barely make out the ski area and a river that they drive past. Somehow, they wind up heading into another state before her father realizes they are going the wrong way. They pass a sign that says, "Scenic View 1 Mile" and her father pulls in.

While he checks the road atlas, Lacey realizes he has started to cry. First it is a few tears trickling down his face. Then stifled weeping. But it keeps coming and coming. "Crescendo," Mrs. Szabo would say if it were a piece of music.

"Oh my God, she doesn't . . . she doesn't. Oh my God. What am I going to do?" Her father whispers to himself, his voice pinched and high like a small child's. He crumples over the steering wheel and buries his head in his folded arms. His shoulders shake as he sobs.

Lacey has never seen her father cry, not even when his mother died. She strokes her rope bracelet and concentrates on her breathing. She glances at Eileen in the rearview mirror. Her sister is sitting up now and their eyes meet.

Lacey puts her index finger in front of her lips and shakes her head. *Don't say anything, don't speak.* She reaches her right hand back behind her seat, grabs Eileen's and squeezes it, and doesn't let go.

Finally, her father stops crying. He wipes his face, breathes deeply with his eyes closed, and counts out loud to ten. "Okay, okay, okay," he says as if he were alone before turning on the radio.

"I think we'll just go straight home." He pats Lacey on her knee, then shifts into reverse. "We were lucky with the rain, weren't we?"

Evidence

THE DOUBLE SWINGING DOORS flap behind you, announcing your presence as you come in out of the oppressive sunlight. The bar is afternoon empty. The few people on stools nod in your general direction. You order a shot of tequila and take your usual spot where the bar slopes around. Right by the bags of chips, pretzels, and the bartender leaning against the bottles.

You always come here by yourself, and while no one quite talks directly to you, you are not left out either. The bartender's brother is always here in the late afternoon with some other guys from his job, cleaning up crime scenes after the L.A.P.D. have taken all the evidence. You started coming pretty regularly on Mondays because they had good stories from the weekend, stories you told yourself you would use in a script someday.

You are here even though it is Thursday, but it's been a bad day. After months of meetings and rewriting a spec script, the television producer finally told you that he's not going to hire you for his new show. Or rather his assistant left a message on your cell phone early this morning thanking you for your interest in the position, which has now been filled.

You swallow the shot, order another one with a beer chaser, and then another. The bartender just looks at you and pours the tequila while moving a toothpick from side to side in his mouth. The place smells strangely comforting, a cross between your grandmother's home and an alley: ammonia, piss, and people who drink so much they sweat liquor. Christmas lights are up all year round, and a variety of beer signs hang on the walls. A few pictures of regulars are scotch-taped to the bar back. You like to tell people you go to this bar. Whenever you drive past with friends, you always point it out.

After your fourth shot, the crime scene cleaners arrive. The bartender puts down his *TV Guide* crossword puzzle, his face loosening as he fills pint glasses, beer spilling onto the counter.

"Hey Frank, what you got for me?" the bartender says to his brother, wiping up the foam with a stained cloth.

"Dead woman eaten by her own dogs." Frank passes around the drinks.

"Her *fifteen* dogs," says one of the cleaners who is bald.

You have another shot and a beer while they describe the dead woman's home. Dog shit everywhere, and they had found dog carcasses and a dead cat in the kitchen. Although she had lived there for years, there were no photographs, barely any furniture, not even a bed.

"We could not figure out where she slept." Frank sucks down his beer.

"I think that was the worst place we've seen," the tall, curly-haired one says.

"What about that fat hoarder who killed himself. Remember the rats in that place?" The bald cleaner stands in front of them. He talks the loudest and always manages to make himself the center of attention.

"Don't even mention him. It took me months to erase that from my memory." Frank shuts his eyes and leans over, while the others laugh.

You are envious of the crime scene cleaners, the combination of routine and horror that is their lives. You wish you had a job with a title, something easy you could tell your mother about and she would understand, instead of explaining over and over that you do actually have an agent and work a lot, but there's never anything to show for it. "I thought you wrote sitcoms," she said when you told her that a special about hair bands you worked on two years ago will finally be on TV. You order another shot, telling yourself not to say these things out loud.

A prostitute who is always here in the late afternoons, like you, monopolizes the jukebox, playing one Journey song after another. She starts arguing with one of the drug dealers who sells coke and crystal meth out of the toilets. As far as you can work out, one of them owes the other money.

You start to have a lot of trouble keeping your head upright and decide to rest it for a minute, but the bartender slams his hand on the bar. "No sleeping."

"Look at the kid," Frank says. They all call you that although you are older than them. "That's impressive, not even six o'clock yet."

"Don't even think about puking on my bar," the bartender says.

You nod at him and then you're on the floor, Frank and the bald cleaner lifting you up. You're not sure how long you've been down, but the prostitute is still shouting, Journey still playing.

"Hey buddy, better get you home," the bald cleaner says. "You live nearby?"

"Sort of," you mumble.

He asks for your car keys. "I'm going to take the kid home," he says to Frank. "Follow me, would ya, in my car?"

You try to make your legs move, but they feel like they have a life of their own and you are merely floating above them. Frank and the bald cleaner each have you by an arm, holding you, leading you out of the bar and down the street towards your car. They open the passenger door and deposit you inside.

"Where you live, buddy?"

You are slumped over but manage to give them the address and rough directions. They slam the door shut, and you watch them confer with each other, look over at you, and laugh.

You pass out, waking up at a stoplight. The radio must be tuned to the classic rock station because Led Zeppelin is playing. "I fucking love this song." The bald cleaner sings along with it, his index fingers beating the air.

You don't even know the name of this man who is driving your car. At each red light, you wake up, your head jerking forward when the car slows down. You keep forgetting where you are and what is happening. You look over again at this strange man. "Who are you?" you ask, unsure if you have really said this, or if it's only a thought. At one point, you feel like you're going to throw up, so he pulls over. But the nausea passes, and you lie back against the headrest, managing to stay awake the rest of the way.

"My girlfriend lives near here," the bald cleaner says, one hand on the steering wheel, the other crooked outside the car window. You think how nice he smells, especially considering what he does all day long. You almost wish you could keep going, drive around all night with him, listening to classic rock. You feel safe with this man you don't know. He looks like he always takes care of everything. He is singing again, and you imagine him doing this while he shaves, right before climbing into bed with his girlfriend. He probably buys her flowers every week, surprises her with gifts when she's least expecting it. The kind of guy who visits his mother on a regular basis, can fix cars and leaking toilets, has a million friends he's known since kindergarten.

And then you are on your street. He pulls up in front of your building. It has never looked shabbier than it does right now. You are thinking of asking him and Frank in for one more drink, not wanting the evening to end quite yet. "The wife is going to kill you, huh, kid?" he says. So you decide against the invite, thank him for the ride, and he hands back your car keys.

Once inside your dark apartment, you walk around, unsure what to do next. You grab a beer, spread out on the couch with the remote and fall asleep. The television is on when you jolt awake, still wearing your jacket, your hand wrapped around the bottle, beer spilled everywhere. Your phone is ringing somewhere. You move over to a dry part of the couch, take off your clothes, and throw them on the floor.

Your desk is in a corner of the room next to a filing cabinet that houses all of your years of work. Spec scripts, sitcom ideas, pilots, game shows, a road trip flick, an unfinished horror movie. Research on hair bands, surfer-punk bands, skater-punk bands, Minneapolis bands, the L.A. scene in the late 1970s, the

Manchester scene in the 1980s, the influence of drugs and rain on music in the latter part of the twentieth century. Except for occasional freelance jobs, no one has seen any of it; no one has sat in a movie theater or on their couch and been entertained or moved by anything you've done. On the floor are the printer and a package of blank paper, waiting for more.

You get up and go to the window. Standing there in your damp boxers, you watch the cars moving between various destinations in the city, people going in and out of the 24-hour convenience store, the laundromat across the street. A glimpse of the sunset filters through palm trees, the only clue that an ocean is a few blocks away. Otherwise you could be anywhere. If everything would stop, just for a moment, you might be able to hear the Pacific, the rhythm of waves breaking apart on land.

Swan Lake

THE MOMENT MAEVE'S UNDERWEAR was down around her ankles in the back seat of Jimmy Flanagan's car, she remembered her little sister, alone in the woods behind the Swan Lake town beach. And the escaped prisoners.

Maeve let out a small groan. Not because of the physical sensation of welcoming Jimmy inside her, the thing she had wanted to happen since glimpsing him in the hallway of Swan Lake Regional High at the start of the year. It was the thought of her ten-year-old sister in the nearby thicket and every wrong decision Maeve had made that day, starting with bringing Molly along to Swan Lake on this unexpected day off from school, in the middle of June.

"Oh, for fuck's sake," Maeve's mother had said the night before, when, driving home from the grocery store, they'd heard on the radio that school was canceled because of the prison escape. Two men doing time for murder had broken out of the maximum-security prison in the adjacent town. They were on foot and presumably in the woods, somewhere close by. "Sorry girls. Shouldn't have said that. But I can't not go to work tomorrow."

Maeve and Molly would have to stay home by themselves, their mother said. With the doors and windows locked. They could go down to the elderly couple who lived on the ground floor of their triple-decker. Otherwise they were to remain inside, even though the forecast for the next day was 85 degrees, with low humidity and clear skies. Even though Maeve's phone vibrated with messages piling in from her friends detailing a plan to spend the entire day at Swan Lake.

Then she got one from Jimmy. *U going*, was all the text said. That was it. Maeve would find a way there. No matter what.

For the first time this school year, Jimmy Flanagan didn't have a girlfriend. It had been several weeks since he had broken up with Dawn Civerelli. Twenty-six days, if you were counting.

"Isn't Molly old enough to stay home by herself?" Maeve tried after dinner as she washed the plates and scrubbed the pots. Her sister was in her bedroom down the hall.

"Not with those animals out there." Her mother was hunched over her phone at the kitchen table, answering work email. "One of them shot a cop twenty-two times, the other guy dismembered his boss." She was whispering, but there was no way Molly could hear her. "Honestly Maeve, you can't go outside. It's not safe. Why do you think they're canceling school? If I had this job longer, I'd stay home with you girls. I hate thinking of you two here, on your own. But I can't call in sick or take a personal day. Not yet at least, that's for sure."

But Maeve was already plotting. She'd simply take Molly with her. There would be at least twenty of them, if not more. They'd be safe. Even at Swan Lake, which was surrounded by woods. The thought of Jimmy, and the possibility of his hands touching her, overruled logic.

"We won't go out, I promise. I'll call you every hour, if that would make you feel better." She squeezed her mother's shoulder to emphasize her point.

In the morning, after their mother left for work, Maeve told her sister about spending the day at the lake. How much fun it would be, but it would have to be a secret. Their secret. Molly listened to the proposal while eating Coco Pops. Leaving the house. Not telling their mother. Breaking the rules.

But it was Maeve who was shaking when they snuck outside, hoping the elderly couple wouldn't hear them in the stairwell, or see the two sisters getting onto their bikes. They pedaled down their quiet, empty street, curtains and shades drawn on all the windows.

Roadblocks were set up on the highways, nighttime curfews imposed, and the police had strongly urged everyone to keep their windows and doors locked at all times. For many, this was a first. Maeve heard people were even sleeping with guns under their pillows.

They crossed Route 20, took a right on Midland Ave. and pedaled until they reached Swan Lake Drive, a dirt road that edged the lake. By the time they reached the town beach, the parking lot was filled with cars. Maeve's friends.

Molly spent the morning swimming with Maeve's two best friends and their boyfriends. Then they made an elaborate sand fort. Maeve lounged on a towel with Jimmy, smoking joint after joint and downing rum and Cokes. Somehow, she remembered to call her mother.

She lay back on Jimmy and he started kissing her neck and she pivoted around so they could embrace. She forgot about Molly, the escaped prisoners, her mother, school, everything in the whole world. Except Jimmy's mouth, Jimmy's tongue, Jimmy's hands, Jimmy's body. People started whistling and jeering, and they took a break to catch their breath and smile at each other.

Then Molly came looking for Maeve, saying she had to go to the bathroom, but the Porta-Johns were locked.

"Just go over there." Maeve pointed vaguely toward the woods. Jimmy snorted.

"Where?" Molly's freckled face scrunched up into a slight scowl.

"You know, back there somewhere."

Molly studied the trees. "Will you come with me?"

"Come on! You don't need me. You can go by yourself."

"I'm scared." Molly looked so young, so much younger than the rest of them.

"Fine." Maeve stood up, stumbling slightly as she walked with her sister into the woods. It was quiet back there, all the noise from the beach turned into a hushed din. Molly squatted down behind a tree.

"You got this, right?" Maeve was trembling for Jimmy.

"Don't go! I'm almost done," Molly pleaded.

But Maeve was already on her way, her pace quickening. The beach was right there after all. When Maeve came into the clearing, Jimmy was waiting for her.

"How about we go hang in my car," he said.

It wasn't until he was on top of her in the back seat that Maeve realized she never actually saw Molly come out of the woods. She waited until Jimmy was finished and then she wriggled from under him and sat up.

"What's wrong?" He pulled up his pants and moved over by the door, facing away from her.

"It's my sister." Maeve was quickly dressing. "I have to find her."

She got out of the car and scanned the beach. Molly wasn't on the sand or out on the raft. That wasn't her with the group hanging off the tire, or with Maeve's two best girlfriends either. Where was she? Maeve paced back and forth, her hand shielding the sun as she looked everywhere. What was she thinking leaving Molly in the woods like that? She could hear her mother shouting at her.

She'd have to go find her. Maeve turned to ask Jimmy if he would come with her, but he was no longer in the car. Instead, he was making his way toward the beach, sauntering through the parked cars, stepping over the wooden barrier that separated the gravelly lot from the swimming area. Without once looking back at her.

Glenn was almost asleep in a deeply air-conditioned room at the Swan Lake Motel off Route 20.

"Do you think there was a point," Rhonda said. "When that woman was making a big meat patty and shaping it around a hacksaw blade that she might have thought, *This is some fucked up shit.*"

Rhonda's words woke him up. "What?" He had no idea what she was talking about.

"The hacksaw blade! She hid it inside frozen meat. You been living under a rock or something?" Rhonda nudged Glenn. "And you're hogging the blankets."

"Sorry. Here." Glenn pushed the orange quilt toward Rhonda and wrapped it around her. "Is that better?" It came out sarcastic, not what he intended.

Rhonda clicked her tongue in disapproval. "You're the only man I know who gets grumpy *after* sex. And please tell me you know about the escaped convicts."

"Of course I know. And I'm really not grumpy. I'm with you. How could I be?"

"What a charmer. Now, where was I? Oh, their lover."

"Lover?"

"The escaped convicts' lover? Who helped the convicts escape? For a lawyer, you're pretty clueless, you know that?"

"It's been a busy week. I try to stay focused on what's really important."

"What, like traffic violations?"

"That is my job, Rhonda. Can I move my arm? It's falling asleep. And how much time have you spent thinking about this, roughly?"

"Everybody except you is thinking about it! It's happening right here." She was shaking her head. "Pass my cigs, will you?"

"Last time I checked, the twentieth century had ended. You can't smoke in motel rooms." He leaned over his side of the bed, grabbed her beige leather bag and passed it to her.

"Oh really?" Rhonda fished around in her purse until she found what she was looking for. She tapped a cigarette out of the pack and lit it up, exhaling a large cloud over the bed. "Well, last time *I* checked, we weren't chopping up a body and you're not paying me. I think that makes us one-percenters compared to the usual Swan Lake Motel customer. I'm having a fucking cigarette!"

"Can I have one then?"

"Ha! You know what your problem is?" Rhonda tossed him the pack and took a large sip of her vodka. The ice made a dull thudding sound as it collided with the thin plastic cup. "You don't really take an interest in things outside of your own life, do you?"

Glenn closed his eyes. Rhonda was a clerk in the traffic court where he went every Tuesday to defend his clients. She had been passing his name along to speeding violators for the better part of a year when he asked if he could buy her a thank-you drink. That was January and they'd been meeting for Friday-afternoon sex ever since. But with each passing week, Rhonda grew more and more irritated with him.

He couldn't seem to do anything right with females these days. Even his twelve-year-old daughter barely made eye contact with him anymore. She would wolf down her breakfast without saying a word, then do the same at dinner. The rest of the time, she was in her room. Occasionally she would ask Glenn why he wasn't a real lawyer, "like Atticus Finch." Only a year ago, she'd been obsessed with baseball, and they'd play catch and follow the Yankees together, checking the scores in the morning, watching games at night and on the weekends. He was going to take her to Yankee Stadium, make a weekend of it in the city. But he'd waited too long. Now she would never agree to go with him.

Then, of course, there was his wife.

"I am interested in things. It's just this prison escape is all Carl talks about." Glenn coughed on his cigarette. His ten-year-old was given to obsessions over breaking news. Carl read everything about the breakout, relaying details to his father as soon as Glenn got home from work. His son kept begging Glenn to drive him over to the prison so he could see all the news trucks, and finally they went last Saturday. "I kind of try to block it out, you know?"

But mentioning his son only made Rhonda angrier. She got up out of bed and began to dress.

"Hey, where are you going?" Glenn's body felt like there was one of those X-ray protective blankets pressing down on him.

"My mother's and then I'm going out." Her eyes were bright with rage. "I have plans tonight."

"Oh. Okay."

"You don't give a shit, do you?"

"About what?"

"Where I'm going or who with or anything. And there is a major event happening right *here*. And it's like it could be on Mars for all you care." She was snapping on her bra. "It's like . . . it's like . . ."

"I'm sorry." He reached for her but she batted his hand away.

She buttoned up her blouse and sat next to him on the bed. "I like you Glenn, I really do. You're a nice guy. But I mean, look at this!" She spread her hands indicating the burnt orange carpet and matching nylon curtains. "We've never made it out of this motel. It's as if we're hiding like those escapees."

Glenn wasn't going to end his marriage, not over this. They both knew that. She kissed his forehead, put on her skirt, and then she was gone.

Glenn fell asleep and didn't wake up until it was dark outside. What would he tell his wife? It would be Glenn's luck if she figured it out, now that the affair was over.

Glenn lay naked between motel sheets. The lights from the cars outside swirled around the room, back and forth, back and forth. From there in the bed, he could see the neon motel sign flickering slightly and the red outline of a swan, its wings spread wide, as if it was about to take flight.

When Georgia woke up with her usual jolt, one thing was clear. She couldn't spend another day barricaded inside the house, alone with her infant. Another beautiful June day with the shades drawn, the doors and windows locked, trolling her laptop while the baby slept, searching for updates about the escaped prisoners. She couldn't do it again. She just couldn't.

She brushed her teeth while Daisy kicked on the pink foot-shaped bathmat. Downstairs, her husband whistled while he made coffee. Then he flipped on the local public radio station.

"Leon," she whispered at her reflection in the mirror above the sink. "What about working at home today?" She practiced the question again, this time with more compulsion, as if it were something they had already discussed. "Leon." Her voice trembled. "Please, Leon."

Her eyes were hallowed out and she was losing her hair. Great clumps of it would come out in her hands when she showered. She looked almost as if she were undergoing chemo, like her best friend who still lived in New York City. They remained close even though it had been fourteen years since Georgia and Leon had left, right after September 11th. Ever since that day, an unease had seeped inside Georgia. It had been her idea to move to Westchester, but they were in the city every day for work. Then they moved to Hudson and mostly telecommuted, but there was a nearby nuclear power plant. Finally, Leon got a job in Plattsburgh and they settled up here, at the very northern end of the Adirondacks. Their house was right on Swan Lake, which seemed like the safest place in the world. The close proximity to the maximum-security prison had never occurred to her, until now.

Since the baby was born seven weeks ago, Georgia had hardly slept more than an hour or two at a stretch. She would sit upright in the middle of the night in a panic. What if Daisy got a fever, or Georgia dropped her, or the baby stopped breathing in her sleep? This amazing beautiful being that Georgia loved more than she thought possible was taking everything from her. Including her sanity.

Leon was home for the first two weeks, and then her mother came. But once she was left on her own, the two men escaped. She knew with certainty that having a baby had been a mistake. What made her think that she possessed the ability to look after a child, raise her and keep her safe? It seemed impossible, especially now with those men somewhere out there.

Daisy gurgled and made cooing noises and Georgia sat on the edge of the tub, burying her face in her hands and wept.

Please Leon, don't leave me here on my own. If she could just have him home for the day. If she could have one morning and one afternoon where she didn't feel scared the whole time. It was only Tuesday and she wasn't sure she would make it until the weekend.

Her husband was careful around her now, treating her like a wild animal that frightened him. When he got home from work in the evening, he would take the baby and make dinner while she had a shower and answered her email. They ate quickly and quietly, taking turns holding the baby or trying to settle her in the infant swing. Daisy seemed calmer around Leon.

Every morning before her husband left for work, she had him check the basement and make sure the padlock was secure on the black steel doors that led out to their backyard. But it didn't make Georgia feel any better. If those men could get out of a maximum-security prison surrounded by barbed wire and armed guards, then it was possible they could find a way into a house that had large picture windows and a plate-glass sliding door.

"They could be anywhere," the governor said at his first press conference about the escape. Those words haunted her. Maybe they were hiding in a closet, waiting for her husband to leave.

She had never seen the prison, even though it was in the next town. With only a couple of convenience stores and a gas station, there was no reason to go there. Now, however, the prison was all she thought about. That and how far two men could get on foot.

"Leon," she whispered yet again, a sob building up in her throat.

Outside, it was sunny and inviting, with puffy, white clouds dotting a blue sky. The kind of day she had imagined when she was pregnant—taking the baby for walks in the nearby park with other new mothers, enjoying lazy picnics at the Swan Lake beach, hosting coffee klatches on her back porch overlooking the water.

Yesterday, the next-door neighbors' dog wouldn't stop barking. A desperate yapping that worsened as the afternoon wore on, only adding to Georgia's feeling of becoming unhinged.

She carried the baby down to the kitchen where Leon, freshly showered in his suit, was packing up his bag for work. She tasted coffee on his lips when he kissed her but she couldn't get the words out. He looked so happy and relieved to be leaving them.

"Wesley, you got a sec? I'm having some family drama." Krystal approached him as he sat in the far corner behind the bar at the Swan Lake Tavern doing the books. Everyone's drinks were refreshed, he noticed. Krystal was the most reliable of his bar staff.

"That doesn't sound good. What is it?" Wesley asked.

"It's Bianca," she groaned. "My stupid sister is bailing on Mom's Fourth of July barbecue. She called last night and was all like, 'There's a part of me that wants to be up there and see the spectacle, not miss out on this piece of history. And then there's another part of me that's too scared to come up.' And then I was waiting for it, for her to say she wasn't coming."

Wesley tried not to show his disappointment at the news. It was fantasies of Bianca that had gotten him through the past couple of months since he and his wife had separated. During Bianca's visit over last year's Fourth of July weekend, Wesley had stayed way past closing time with her one night, listening intently while she explained the intricacies of being a flight attendant, that she could deliver a baby *and* hogtie someone to their seat. She knew how to perform CPR, make a tourniquet, and use every piece of emergency equipment stored in the overhead compartments at the back of the cabin, including the defibrillator, needles, emergency repairs. "Pushing that cart up and down the aisle is the least of what I do," she said. Then they made out in the parking lot.

No one knew Wesley's wife had kicked him out a month before the prisoners escaped and that he'd been sleeping on a friend's couch ever since. He kept it from Krystal and the other bartenders, the waitresses, and the kitchen crew. Even his business partner. And he certainly didn't mention it to the customers, a regulars crowd partial to late afternoons, early evenings, and televised sports. As the night wore on, tempers had been known to flare with enough frequency to warrant keeping a baseball bat behind the bar.

The prison outbreak had been good for business though, there was no doubt about it. The place was heaving during lunch with plenty of first-timers who ended up staying on into the afternoon to watch the 24-hour local news coverage on the televisions framing the bar and the large screen that dominated a wall in the main dining area. Phones beeped and buzzed with alerts all day. On the rare occasions that there was a development in the story—like the sighting along the Pennsylvania border that turned out to be false, or the discovery of a bloody sock in a hunting cabin—the bar would come to a standstill. The only sounds would be glasses lifted to lips and put back down onto paper coasters. Krystal, who bartended weekday lunches and afternoons, would add another pushpin on the map taped to the wall, marking each significant development in the story. She put the map up on the first day of the prison escape. Like they do on cop shows, she said. Mostly though, nothing happened and they were stuck watching loops of police roadblocks and B-roll of the prison.

"Mom's crushed," Krystal said. "I mean, Bianca can fly here for free. That's the best part of being a flight attendant, she says. She can come home a lot. But her five times a year visits have dwindled down to one, the Fourth, and now, not even that. And poor Mom invited the neighbors, her book club, the women she plays mahjong with. "My Bianca is coming home," she's been telling everyone. Typical fucking Bianca."

Wesley kept his face neutral. He didn't need Krystal figuring out that he had feelings for her sister.

"And I know I told you I'd work lunch on the Fourth, but is there any way I could take the whole day off? I feel like I need to be at my mom's all day, not just the evening party part."

Wesley had no plans for the Fourth, or for the rest of the summer for that matter. He assured her that it was no problem at all.

"Oh man, Wesley, I owe you big time," she said and turned her attention to the customers to see who needed a refill.

Charlie indicated his empty glass. He was at his usual stool, three down from Wesley, where he would remain well into the evening until he couldn't hold his head up any longer. Then someone would have to call his daughter to come take him home. Krystal poured out two fingers of whiskey neat and put it in front of him.

"They think Vern's involved with this thing," he said. "Helped with the escape. Dumb as a pound of dumb he is. That's a Maine saying, by the by."

"I heard the same thing about Vern," Eammon drained his glass, leaving behind a foamy Guinness residue. He rarely missed a day at the bar. "He was bringing in screwdrivers for one of them. Or some crazy shit like that."

"My money is on organized crime." Bill made patterns with empty peanut shells. He'd actually seen the two men right after they escaped while drinking his 6:00 a.m. cup of coffee. They were standing by his kids' old rusted jungle gym. But the news hadn't broken yet. So all Bill did was holler at them from his back porch, dressed only in his bathrobe, asking what in the hell they thought they were doing. They were lost, one of them explained, and they apologized and hurried off. It wasn't until a few hours later when Bill heard about the escape on the radio that he put it together. Must have been no more than thirty feet away from them, he told the crowd at the bar later that afternoon.

Bill gave his vodka tonic a shake. "If not the Mafia per se, then definitely a drug gang. No way they did this by their selves."

"They are still here somewhere, I bet." Krystal was moving quickly, refilling drinks. "I can feel it."

"No way. They must be in Canada by now. Laughing at us fools," Charlie said. "I mean, how could they not get to Canada? It's right fucking there."

Krystal put out bowls of mini pretzels and peanuts. "My boyfriend rigged up our place with so many guns, one of us is gonna get killed, I swear. He walks around with one in his holster, even to go to the toilet!"

"What are you still doing with that nut job?" Eammon shook his head.

With all the drama unfolding, it was easy for Wesley to pretend to himself that his life was the way it used to be, filled with dull routines like the school morning rush of eating breakfast, scraping soggy remnants of his three children's barely touched cereal into the garbage, making lunches, hair being brushed, frantic searches for homework and library books and shin guards, socks that matched or weren't itchy. Always running late, and many mornings there were tears. His children used to bicker about the music as he drove them to school, or whose turn it was to sit up front, or any number of other small grievances. By the time they had finished the ten-minute drive, Wesley's head would be throbbing. Why was being with his children so soul-destroying, he would wonder as he made his way over for a quick stop with one of the handful of women he was sleeping with.

Now, though, his mornings were quiet, empty spaces, one long blob of time. His children had become strangers and when he was with them, it felt like babysitting someone else's kids. They would sit in the back seat of the car quietly. No one wanted to listen to music, or sit up front with him, or do much of anything that involved interacting with their father. It was like they were in the waiting room at the dentist, just enduring the time with Wesley, until they could get back to their real lives.

Wesley wasn't sure he could hide his disappointment about Bianca much longer, so he gathered up his paperwork and laptop and headed to the back of the restaurant. His longing for Bianca had gotten him through some lonely months. He had even allowed himself to start thinking of a future with her. Maybe she was the woman he was supposed to be with. But she never told him that she wasn't coming, and her emails were becoming less and less frequent.

The tables in back were mostly empty, except for the elderly couple who frequented the Swan Lake Tavern most days for lunch, ordering the same thing each time. They sat at a table in the far corner by the windows, and from the looks of it, spent most of their meal sparring. Wesley thought of them as the ghost of Christmas future, and it was his fear of turning into them that had partially propelled him to act so badly towards his wife. It seemed like the worst thing he could imagine. Being a boring, old couple who only argued with nothing nice left to say to one another.

"Some people dye their hair white. They like the way it looks," the woman said. "A lot of money they pay for it. You know, to get it that color."

"Why would you spend money to look old?" her husband asked.

"People's views are changing on that. Something to celebrate now, they say."

"What's to celebrate? Who in their right mind actually likes sagging chins and bellies? And you got your aching back, and sickness, body parts giving out, friends dying. And the hair. Either you are losing it or it turns that ugly color."

"You're impossible, you know that," the woman said.

"Isn't that what you love about me? You know I think you're beautiful, don't you?"

Wesley looked over at the couple. They were holding hands and there was a bottle of Korbel Brut in an ice bucket next to a bouquet of red roses.

"Even after all these years?"

"Especially so. Here's to sixty more years, my love. And pass the champagne, would you? Let's have another toast. To you, my beautiful wife."

Sunlight refracted through the champagne bottle on the table, spreading a green glow over the couple's intertwined fingers.

It was Cassidy's idea that she and Jocelyn should find the escaped prisoners themselves. She was certain they were here, in the Swan Lake Campground and RV Park. It was the perfect hiding place, only a few miles from the prison and the police would never think of it. It was too obvious, Cassidy reckoned. If she and Jocelyn found them, there'd be big money in it, and they'd be famous. Way more famous even than the two men.

Jocelyn would never have met Cassidy if her cousins had come on the annual family camping trip. But after the escape, her mother's three sisters and their families decided not to come. Jocelyn heard her parents arguing the merits versus the risks. In the end, because her father had already booked the time off, and they couldn't afford to go anywhere else, they decided to still come.

The first morning of the trip, Jocelyn thought she would die of boredom. Usually, there were twelve of them riding their bikes barefoot to the beach, the playground, or just racing around and around the campground. They would play Manhunt in the dark with flashlights, team hide-and-seek, Witchiepoo, super-heroes. Each year, they went tubing on the Swan River, which fed into the lake, climbed Swan Lake Mountain, hiked to the waterfalls, and went on a day trip to Frontier Town. It was Jocelyn's favorite week of the year.

This summer though, the campground was mostly empty. The trails and outdoor recreational areas were all closed. Posters of the two men were everywhere. Jocelyn and her younger brothers weren't allowed any electronics, but this week her parents caved. Her brothers whiled away the mornings playing games on their parents' phones.

When Jocelyn met Cassidy at the camping store in the late afternoon of their second, very long day, it felt like her luck was beginning to change. Within hours, they were best friends in only the way that bored girls can become. Even though Cassidy was two years older. Especially because of that. Cassidy had been living in an RV in the campground since April with her mother and her mother's new boyfriend. Before that, it was a trailer park outside Buffalo with a different boyfriend. And last fall, it had been Central Ohio. Cassidy said her mother wanted to stay on the road forever, and if they kept going, her father would never find them. When Jocelyn's mother told her not to hang out with *that girl*, wrinkling up her nose, it only cemented Jocelyn's devotion to her new friend.

It was Jocelyn's last day and as usual, the girls were

sunning themselves in a corner of the beach, as far away from Jocelyn's family as they could get. Jocelyn loved the pinched look on her mother's face when she'd come over each day to say that lunch was ready. "Not hungry," Jocelyn would tell her, as she lay spread out with magazines and suntan oil and a makeup bag that belonged to Cassidy's mother.

Cassidy leaned up on her elbows and plotted how she and Jocelyn were going to solve the country's biggest mystery. This was their chance to do something meaningful with their lives, she said. Jocelyn was uneasy about it, but she didn't want to disappoint Cassidy. If she went to Jocelyn's middle school, all the boys would be in love with her, and all the girls with perfect hair would want to be like her. Those girls never even looked at Jocelyn, let alone talked to her. Spending time with a girl like Cassidy seemed like a once-in-a-lifetime opportunity.

All week Cassidy had doled out wisdom as they lay on their towels. That a flat stomach was the key to a boy's heart. And she should know. Already broken fifteen of them. Tee shirts should be tied or cut so your stomach is exposed. Always. But you have to do at least fifty sit-ups a day to keep your stomach flat. It also pushes up your breasts and makes them look bigger, helps give you really good cleavage. Jocelyn had only small lumps and cleavage seemed like a dream that would never happen. Also, boys like girls who smoke. Signals that you put out. And use your tongue when you kiss them. "I can show you how to do it," Cassidy offered, but Jocelyn declined.

Cassidy wasn't afraid of anything. Not even the escaped convicts. If she did encounter them in the woods surrounding the Swan Lake Campground, well, she'd head off with them. Help them hotwire her mother's car. Nothing sounded better than driving all the way to Mexico with them.

"I can talk anyone into anything," she said.

They made lunch in Cassidy's trailer, bologna with mayonnaise on white bread that was so soft, it felt like wet toilet paper in Jocelyn's mouth. Cassidy's mother shouted at her daughter, her eyes half-open, her words slurry. There were scabs all up and down her arms, same as her boyfriend who leered at Cassidy and Jocelyn while they ate. Then they returned to the beach and came up with the details of their plan to find the escaped prisoners.

Cassidy said the two men who were staying in the grey pup tent at the very far end of the campground must be the escapees. The girls would meet at midnight by the bathrooms. There was a full moon so they wouldn't even need flashlights. They'd set up a stake out and wait until the men went somewhere in the morning. Then they could sneak into their tent and gather evidence. Once they had enough proof, they could go to the police.

If Jocelyn had shown up, maybe all the things Cassidy had talked about would have come true. Fur coats and limousines and walking the red carpet at the premiere of the movie based on their lives and Oprah and the cover of *People*. Instead, when her alarm went off on her phone, Jocelyn remained in her sleeping bag next to her brothers, listening to her parents snoring in the next tent. She didn't have it in her to do any of the things that she and Cassidy had talked about. Find the convicts. Get boys. Be something that she really wasn't.

She lay perfectly still as Cassidy hissed at her outside the tent. "Come on, Jocelyn. Come on."

Her brothers sighed and squirmed in their sleep.

"You're pathetic, Jocelyn. A total wuss. I should have known better than to waste my time with you."

In the morning, Jocelyn would go home, back to her real life. Where no one cared about her good grades, her swimming medals, or that each summer she read the most books in the town library challenge. Everything would be exactly the same. She heard Cassidy's footsteps walking away, and just like that, the opportunity to finally be noticed vanished altogether.

The two men never went to Swan Lake, or to any of the

towns near the prison they had escaped from. Instead, they made their way through the deep woods for twenty-three days before being caught. One didn't survive.

Molly was obsessed with the escaped prisoners from the beginning, from the very first day of the breakout. She clipped articles from the local papers and pasted them into a notebook, making sure they were dated and in chronological order. Every morning she woke up to the news on her clock radio, hoping for updates on their whereabouts, insisted that her mother let her watch the news while she ate breakfast, hurried home from school to find out what had happened while she was gone.

After it was all over, the newspapers detailed how the men hid out in hunting cabins, surviving on stolen food and liquor, but eventually split up because they were arguing so much. What was it like though, when they were together, just the two of them with the whole world searching for them? This was the part of the story that fascinated Molly. But the newspapers didn't have many details beyond the actual escape. In fact, they missed out on so much. Like the day the area schools were closed. The local papers had pictures of teenagers hanging out at Swan Lake—their mother confronted Maeve about it and she insisted they had been home all day.

But those articles said nothing about how Maeve left Molly in the woods. How she'd hid behind a large oak for close to an hour, too scared to move at all, and didn't hear her sister calling for her, only twigs snapping, insects reverberating off the trees, the beach sounds far enough away that no one would be able to hear her scream, if she needed to. How it was like one of her nightmares where she couldn't get her legs to work and the killer was getting closer and closer.

And when Maeve finally did find her, they hugged for a long time, both weeping, Maeve saying over and over that she was sorry, and Molly felt happy. Finally, her sister was paying attention to her. Her older sister who never had time for Molly anymore. Not since they moved up to Swan Lake last year and Maeve was always off with her friends while Molly spent most afternoons at home by herself, sometimes so lonely that she'd resort to hanging out with the old, annoying couple on the ground floor.

Once they were reunited, the sisters rode their bikes home, and spent the rest of the afternoon inside their apartment, like they were supposed to. Maeve made them popcorn which they ate while sitting together on the sofa, watching television and drinking sodas. They watched game shows, old black and white comedies, *Keeping Up With the Kardashians*. They avoided the news altogether.

Now that the news trucks were gone and the rest of the country had moved on to other things, other stories, Molly sat at her desk looking at the articles and all the missing information. She turned to a blank page in her notebook and picked up her pen. And then she began.

Acknowledgments

Since college, it has been my dream to publish a collection of short stories. There are so many people who made this dream possible. First and foremost, I want to thank Martha Rhodes, director of Four Way Books, for accepting this book for publication and sending me possibly the best email I have ever received. The dream continued with her expert editing and kindness and the opportunity to work with the equally talented and kind Sally Ball, Katie Berta, Mari Coates, Clarissa Long, Ryan Murphy, and everyone at Four Way Books.

I want to thank my teachers, starting with the late Jane Prescott, who was both my kindergarten and fourth grade teacher, for giving me a life-long love of reading and writing and who always made me feel like I was special and that what I had to say was important. I have had so many amazing writing teachers over the years, and I learned so much from each one, including the writers that I only had the chance to study with briefly. The following writers were especially helpful in providing feedback on these stories and/or sharing their knowledge about the craft of writing and their enthusiasm for it: Lynda Barry, Dan Chaon,

Nicholas Christopher, Elizabeth England, Elizabeth Gaffney, Mary Gaitskill, John Reed and Patrick Ryan. And a special thank you to Will Allison whose incredible editing took these stories to another level. I am so grateful for your expertise and careful eye, and also for teaching me so much about short stories and revision.

The Virginia Center for the Creative Arts has provided early and continued support of my writing, and I am particularly grateful to Sheila Gulley Pleasants, deputy director/director of artists' services, for her extremely hard work in making VCCA such a supportive atmosphere and so conducive to creativity and community. I learned so much from the writers, artists, and composers I met during my residencies there; thank you for sharing your projects with me and your ideas about art and creativity. The Writers Room in New York City and the local history wing of the Berkshire Athenaeum Public Library in Pittsfield, Massachusetts, provided a quiet oasis where these stories were written and revised.

Thank you to the many editors of literary magazines and curators at reading series who have supported my work over many years, including: *3:AM*, *Atticus Review*, *Bound Off*, *Epiphany*, *Failbetter*, *FictionNow*, the Guerrilla Lit Reading Series, *LOST*, and the Million Writers Award. And thank you to the entire New York City Listen to Your Mother team from 2013 and 2017, most especially Amy Wilson and Kizz Robinson. The opportunity to present my writing to a larger audience and the support and expertise you provided was life-changing.

I am grateful to my various work "families" over the years, especially *Spy*, *Ms.*, City Project, Community-Word Project, Teachers & Writers Collaborative, and the DreamYard Project, where I learned so much about storytelling, writing, collaboration, research, editing, meeting deadlines, and fact-checking. An extra thank you to my colleagues from *Ms.*; that was such a special time in my life, we were truly a family, and I am so thankful for the opportunity to work with you all.

Thank you to my teaching artist colleagues for support and inspiration, especially David Ciminello, Andrea Greene, Ellen Hagan, Elizabeth Hamilton, Abigail Hastings and Renée Watson. A special thank you to all of the classroom teachers, social workers, administrators, and school security guards I have worked with over the years, most especially Deonna Gould and Michelle Jervis-White; your dedication, hard work, and love for your students is awe-inspiring. To all of the hundreds and hundreds of students that I have taught over the years, thank you for sharing your stories with me. And a huge thank you to the incarcerated women at Bedford Hills Correctional Facility who have attended my writing workshops; thank you for trusting me with your words. You have had a huge impact on me, and it is truly an honor to hear your amazing writing. There is nothing like entering a classroom with blank pieces of paper and then leaving with new poems written in a noisy, overcrowded classroom, the inside of a juvenile detention facility, or a maximum-security prison, that demonstrates the power and importance of the written word.

I had the good fortune to be in a ten-year-plus writing workshop with Jennifer Cooke, Abigail Hastings, Alice Naude, and Jody Winer, who helped me so much with these stories, encouraged me, and kept me going. None of these stories would have been written without you four. I want to thank the many other people I have been in writing workshops with over the years, especially Carolyn Goldhush, Jason Lees, Bernard Lumpkin, Katie Rogin, and Judy Warner.

I am grateful to the many parents and teachers at my daughters' schools and after-school programs for providing love and support to our family, most especially: Charlotte Arnoux, Robin Burchill, Katie Cappiello, Liz Craig, Charly Green, Jennie Miller, Susie Page, Lisa Pilato, Theseus Roche, Allison Schoen, Shino Tanikawa, Sheri von Seeburg, and the late Bill Gerstel and Susan Korn.

I am extremely lucky to have friendships that span decades. Writing these stories involved so much self-doubt and time alone, wondering what I was doing, and I wouldn't have been able to do it without the following outstanding, incredible people:

Richard Arthur, Moira Brennan, Steve Brown, José Carlos Casado, Ivy Dane, Barbara Findlen, Meredith Fuchs, Jay Gardner, Anne Gisleson, Kristen Golden, Judy Goldschmidt, Catherine Gund, Jeanne Koenig, Jeff Magness, Colleen McCabe, Justin Morreale, Billy Morrissette, Sujean Rim, Filemon Rodriguez, Keith Summa, Richard Shepard, Maura Tierney, Megan Tingley, and Dan Zevin. I cannot come up with adequate words to thank you all enough for everything.

A special thank you to: Keith, for my author photo but most especially for still talking to me after my awkward introduction during that life-changing Nicholas Christopher writing class in the fall of 1985—how diminished my life would be if you had made the (totally reasonable) decision that I was just too weird; Jay, for the beautiful cover photograph and for being the best neighbor ever; and Meredith, for taking time on the morning of your wedding to sit me down and say that if I really wanted to be a writer, I needed to get way more serious about it.

To my nieces and nephews, I so cherish my time with you and your lovely partners; your friendship as well as your support of my writing means so much to me. And to my goddaughter, Petra, who has helped make all the painful events that have happened since

January 2016 easier to deal with because now you are in the world.

Thank you to Pat and Ernie Blackman for always believing in me as a writer and for sharing your own amazing stories with me. One of the luckiest parts of my life is to have you both as bonus extra parents.

Thank you to Stephen, king of brothers, and Janet, queen of sisters, for love and support and your devotion to spending so much time together, and that our children can have such a strong sense of family.

To my parents who read to me when I was little and instilled in me their deep love for books and writing, and have done everything for me and my siblings. Despite painful losses in their own childhoods, they were able to provide me and my siblings a great one filled with love and security and, of course, books, and who are the best parents ever.

Thank you to my daughters for everything. Getting to be your mom is the greatest privilege in the whole world. I was writing before you were born, but I wasn't really a writer until your arrival. I am certain that I have learned so much more from you both than the other way around. And to Andy: I can't imagine my life if you hadn't taken my number on the mid-level platform at Holborn tube station in August 1987, if I hadn't run into Steve and Kim in the middle of Washington Square Park two months later, and then again outside the movie theater the following summer. Three chance encounters have given me everything that is amazing and extraordinary in my life.

Finally, for my life-long friend Marsh McCall, who taught me so much about storytelling and humor and most especially love, and is gone much too soon. I am so grateful to Stella, Murphy, Jasa and Marsh's family for keeping me in your lives and continuing to share our stories of Marsh.

Many of these stories were previously published, some in different formats or with different titles, in the following publications: *Atticus Review*, *decomP*, *Epiphany*, *Failbetter*, *FictionNow*, *KGB Bar Lit Magazine*, and *LOST*.

Susan Buttenwieser's writing has appeared in numerous publications. *We Were Lucky with the Rain* is her first book. She teaches creative writing in New York City public schools and to incarcerated women.

Publication of this book was made possible by grants and donations. We are also grateful to those individuals who participated in our 2019 Build a Book Program. They are:

Anonymous (14), Sally Ball, Vincent Bell, Jan Bender-Zanoni, Laurel Blossom, Adam Bohannon, Lee Briccetti, Jane Martha Brox, Anthony Cappo, Carla & Steven Carlson, Andrea Cohen, Janet S. Crossen, Marjorie Deninger, Patrick Donnelly, Charles Douthat, Morgan Driscoll, Lynn Emanuel, Blas Falconer, Monica Ferrell, Joan Fishbein, Jennifer Franklin, Sarah Freligh, Helen Fremont & Donna Thagard, Ryan George, Panio Gianopoulos, Lauri Grossman, Julia Guez, Naomi Guttman & Jonathan Mead, Steven Haas, Bill & Cam Hardy, Lori Hauser, Bill Holgate, Deming Holleran, Piotr Holysz, Nathaniel Hutner, Elizabeth Jackson, Rebecca Kaiser Gibson, Dorothy Tapper Goldman, Voki Kalfayan, David Lee, Howard Levy, Owen Lewis, Jennifer Litt, Sara London & Dean Albarelli, David Long, Ralph & Mary Ann Lowen, Jacquelyn Malone, Fred Marchant, Donna Masini, Louise Mathias, Catherine McArthur, Nathan McClain, Richard McCormick, Kamilah Aisha Moon, James Moore, Beth Morris, John Murillo & Nicole Sealey, Kimberly Nunes, Rebecca Okrent, Jill Pearlman, Marcia & Chris Pelletiere, Maya Pindyck, Megan Pinto, Barbara Preminger, Kevin Prufer, Martha Rhodes, Paula Rhodes, Silvia Rosales, Linda Safyan, Peter & Jill Schireson, Jason Schneiderman, Roni & Richard Schotter, Jane Scovell, Andrew Seligsohn & Martina Anderson, Soraya Shalforoosh, Julie A. Sheehan, James Snyder & Krista Fragos, Alice St. Claire-Long, Megan Staffel, Marjorie & Lew Tesser, Boris Thomas, Pauline Uchmanowicz, Connie Voisine, Martha Webster & Robert Fuentes, Calvin Wei, Bill Wenthe, Allison Benis White, Michelle Whittaker, Rachel Wolff, and Anton Yakovlev.